mina's spring of colors

mina's spring of colors

RACHNA GILMORE

FITZHENRY & WHITESIDE

First published in the United States in 2000.

Fitzhenry & Whiteside acknowledges with thanks the support of the Government of Canada through its Book Publishing Industry Development Program.

Printed in Canada.
Book Design by: alter

10 9 8 7 6 5 4

Canadian Cataloguing in Publication Data

Gilmore, Rachna, 1953 - Mina's spring of colors

ISBN 1-55041-549-2 (bound)   ISBN 1-55041-534-4 (pbk.)

I. Title.

PS8563.I57M56 2000   jC813'.54   C00-930531-9
PZ7.G54Mi 2000

Dedication:
For Karleen Bradford, Jan Andrews, Alice Bartels and
Caroline Parry – partners in fiction, friends and bon vivants.

Acknowledgements:
I thank the Multiculturalism Program of the Department
of Canadian Heritage for their support and
financial assistance.

I also thank my family: Ian for his unfailing support and
encouragement; Karen and Robin for their interest, their
many useful suggestions and for making sure that my
characters don't "speak geek."

As well, I would like to thank my publisher, Gail Winskill
and my agent Melanie Colbert for their encouragement,
enthusiasm and faith in my work; and Charis Wahl for her
bullseye editing, her pungent sense of humour and for never
letting me get away with anything. Thanks also to Bina
Suterwala for providing me with background information
about Holi and her interest in my work. And of course,
finally, thanks to all the friends who cheer me on through
the vagaries of the writing life and pretend to be
interested, even when I obsess and fixate endlessly.

mina's spring of colors

chapter one

"Mina?"

Oh, great! I stop channel surfing, mute the TV and scrunch down on the couch.

"Minakshi."

I thunk my head back on the cushion. He never gives up.

Nanaji's face peers over the top of the couch. His glasses reflect the TV screen — some dancers on a music video.

"There you are Minu." He says it in Hindi. He talks to me in Hindi a lot of the time. I always talk in English. He wags a finger. "What? Are you hiding from me?"

I smile politely. He's my grandfather and I love him and everything, but...

Nanaji's smile fades. "Now what is so entertaining about this? Look at it — are you aware of the message it is really sending? Why don't you turn it off, Mina, do something productive."

"But Nanaji, I just got home from school, and I was only flicking around — it's not a big deal." I try not to sound annoyed but my voice comes out squeaky.

"Not a big deal," Nanaji repeats it in English. It sounds so — awkward. He goes on in Hindi, eyes twinkling. "Your mind could turn to mush and that's not a big deal? How will you think with por-ridge for brains?"

I make a small face.

"Come. Turn it off, there's nothing good on. Let's play our math game." Nanaji's eyes gleam.

No. Not another math game — mental arith-metic is not my idea of fun. But I reach for the remote control. "All right, I'll turn it off." I know I sound grumpy, but I don't care.

Nanaji rubs my head. "That's it. Now let's—"

"I've got tons of homework, Nanaji; I don't have time for games."

"Ah, homework. All right, but if you finish soon, we can play." He chuckles. "See who's faster this time."

"I can't." I fumble in my head for an excuse. Not the board game I'm making — he doesn't think that's *productive*. Got it! "I have to make invitations for our Holi party. On the computer. Mom and Dad want them ready for Friday."

He'll be fine with that — Nanaji thinks it's great that we celebrate Holi, the Festival of Color, and he knows nothing about computers. Good thing he hasn't figured out I can play games on it.

"Okay, go, go. Get started."

He tries to hug me as I go past. I pretend not to notice and run past him.

Up in my room, I flop down at my desk. It's covered with the purple cards I'm writing out for my roller-coaster game. I pick them up, one by one, put them in a pile.

That look in his eyes — was it sort of hurt? Maybe I should have given him a hug. It wouldn't have been that big a deal, just to have given him a hug...I slap down the last card.

Why should I feel bad about it? What does he expect — that I'm going to be his shadow, like when I was little?

I was only seven that last time we visited him in India. Boy, was I ever a nerd. I used to cling to him, totally crack up over his jokes. I couldn't get enough of his stories, especially the ones about the blue god Krishna, the mischief he got up to as a kid — I used to beg Nanaji for more. And how I bawled on the train when we had to leave.

I knock over the pile of cards. Yeah, well, I'm not a seven-year-old dweeb anymore.

I can't believe I actually thought it would be cool to have him living with us. It's been four months, but it feels like forever.

He'd been living with Mom's brother, Uncle Suresh, in India, but when Uncle Suresh got transferred to Kenya, Mom insisted Nanaji come and stay with us. She was worried about his heart condition and getting good medical care.

All I thought about was finally getting to stay home instead of going to Celeste's after school. No more waiting, all tired and fed up when Mom and Dad were both late at work. No more feeling weird and awkward around those babies. I mean, I was the oldest kid there, I'm eleven; I sure don't need a baby sitter. But Mom's got this thing about latch-key kids and anyway, it's supposed to be the law that you can't leave kids under twelve alone, even though lots of people do.

Did I ever have big plans! TV — what I wanted to watch, not the kiddy stuff at Celeste's. Time to work on my board games. Eating what I wanted instead of boring old celery and cheese sticks, maybe even some junk food — yeah, right.

I scratch an extra smear of blue oil pastel off my roller-coaster game.

It's not that I don't love Nanaji — I do. It's just that he's always at me. *Be aware, know who you really are. Aware* is his favorite word. And *productive*. He used to be a philosophy professor in India. I don't care that he still reads those heavy, old Indian books, the Vedas, but why does he have to try and get me interested? One time I asked about his book and he got started on how my true self was really the eye of the eye, the ear of the ear! Puh-leeze!

I pick at the blue under my fingernail.

There's a messy knot in the middle of my chest. It feels kind of awful thinking about Nanaji like this. When I was little, it was so easy — I loved being around him.

But now, I wish…I wish he'd never moved here. There. I've said it.

chapter two

A bit of math homework and then the corrections to my English test. I rush through them, then slowly, carefully, color in two more squares for my roller-coaster game. Bright purple and yellow in oil pastel crayons — it's going to be awesome, my best game ever. Jess thinks it's way better than even my Surviving School game.

Nanaji, of course, thinks it's a total waste of time, even though he never comes right out and says so. I mean, the people who thought up Trivial Pursuit made a freaking fortune. Wait 'til I make a million bucks, then he'll see.

When I'm done, I creep downstairs. Nanaji is puttering in the kitchen. Good. He doesn't see me.

As I sneak toward the study, where the computer is, I hear something sizzling. Ginger and garlic smells sting inside my nose.

Another thing Nanaji's taken over — cooking.

When he came here, Nanaji hadn't cooked in years, not since he was a student in England — in India they had servants for *everything*. But when he saw how late Mom and Dad work, he went at it.

Okay, so it's nice that he wants to help, but the way Mom goes on about it... We don't have servants but Michèle comes in every week to clean, and what's the big deal with cooking anyway? Dad used to sling together nachos on his night to cook, and a lot of the time we'd order pizza or Chinese. But now it's Indian food, Indian food, Indian food. It's not that I don't like Indian food, but it's been ages since we've had Mom's spaghetti.

I slip the *Do Not Disturb* sign on the doorknob and shut the door. Too bad there isn't a lock.

I turn on the computer and play Hangman and FreeCell. I keep an ear open for footsteps. If Nanaji finds out about the games he'll be checking up on me all the time.

I'm just about to win at FreeCell when there's a tapping on the door.

"Minakshi?"

Quickly, I minimize the FreeCell and click on the Spring Bash file. Last year's invitation comes up on the screen.

Nanaji opens the door. "Ha, working, I see."

"Yeah, I'm going to add more colors, make everything spring-like."

Nanaji shakes his head. "It's amazing, this computer-shomputer. Mmm. But it makes you more productive."

I roll my eyes slightly. And feel kind of mean — but it's not like he can see. I turn around anyway and smile at him.

He comes closer and reads the top of the screen. "Very nice. *The Annual Salvi Family Spring Bash. A Celebration of Holi, The Festival of Colors.*"

My back prickles. The way he pronounces the English words — Mom doesn't talk like that, even though she was born in India. She's always spoken English and has only the teeniest bit of an Indian accent. Dad hasn't any — he went to school here. Nanaji says that Dad's Hindi has a funny accent. I can't be bothered, I quit Hindi school years ago.

Nanaji is reading on, silently. "Good, good, you have an explanation of Holi. Did you write that?"

"As if, Nanaji! It's all big words like a magazine article. No, Mom did."

It sounds so stiff — in a way, the total opposite of Holi. I don't know why she always puts it in, everyone already knows about it. Mom says it's for the new people we invite but there's no one new in my class — except for Ashley. I look through it quickly.

Holi is the Festival of Color, celebrated in India. It is played in the spring, usually February or March, but we are celebrating it later to accommodate our weather. During Holi, people shower each other with colored powders called "gulal," either dry or mixed with water. It's a wonderful free-for-all, a rejoicing for the winter harvest and the arrival of spring. The throwing of the colored powders symbolizes the letting go of old quarrels and animosities. As well, the colors represent the personality taking on a different hue: the changing of old hatreds to positive, brighter feelings. It is a time to bring together all people, old and young, rich and poor. No one is exempt. Join us for the fun — if you dare!

Nanaji smiles. "Oh-ho, I'm really looking forward to it — my first time playing Holi here with you."

The palms of my hands go tingly and whirly every time I think of Holi.

"But what happens at the party?"

"Oh, we put tables all around the yard, with plates and plates of powders. Mom and Dad get tons of it.

And also squirt bottles — you know, the ones in the garage — we get them all ready with the powder mixed with water the night before. It's so fun, Jessie always comes over to help."

Nanaji's eyes twinkle.

"And for the party, lots of people bring their own bottles. Sometimes it's really weird — like food coloring, or beet water." I grin at him. "It doesn't always wash out."

Nanaji chuckles.

"So, when everyone's here, Mom makes her little speech and then..." I bounce in my chair, "everyone goes at it."

Nanaji shakes his head. "In India, of course, it's different. People playing Holi in the streets, any-where. You can target anyone — what fun! I wish you could see that."

My smile wipes off. What's our party? Nothing?

Nanaji pats my head. "But, here, of course, this is best. Very nice, Mina. I'll let you finish. Don't take too long, we have to eat soon. Your mummyji and daddyji should be home anytime."

He always adds *ji* to their names, even though it's used mostly for older people — it's supposed to be a sign of respect.

Nanaji goes on, "There is your open house at the school, don't forget. We have to get ready."

The open house. I swing around and blurt, "Are you coming?"

"Of course. I want to see your classroom, your work." Nanaji shuts the door behind him.

Nanaji at the open house. Okay, so I don't mind him seeing my school but...all my friends will be there. What if he tries to start a math game? Or goes on about being aware?

Should I try to talk him out of it? Get him to stay home?

He looked so eager. I can't do it, I can't; it would be so mean. Anyway, Mom and Dad would get really mad. I'll just...just have to keep away from him.

Maybe it won't be so bad. Hopefully, Nanaji will get talking to Jessie's dad. Mr. Henley's interested in the same stuff. They always have these long boring conversations.

Anyway, Jess and I aren't going to be with our families. We'll hang out with the kids — come to think of it, we'll probably be swamped.

I grin. It's not that I'm one of the super-popular kids; I'm kind of somewhere in the middle. Except for this time of the year — everyone wants to come to our Spring Bash.

Even Ashley. She thinks she's so cool because her parents let her buy clothes from the Gap, and everyone thinks she's so gorgeous. She never bothered with me until she found out about the Holi party. I mean, her dad and my mom work together in the same engineering firm, but she still pretty well ignored me. The only person she had any time for was Samantha, who's just like her. I don't know *what* the boys see in them.

But now Ashley's falling over herself to be friendly. She even waits for Jess and me at her front gate and walks to school with us.

Craig, too. Normally, he avoids girls like poison, but he actually gave me a bookmark. Okay, so it was covered with guns and monsters, but he thought it was wonderful. And he hasn't called me or Jessie *dipwad* or *nark* all month.

I bet he found out about last year. I didn't want to invite him or some of the other creepy little boys he hangs out with. Except Mom insisted. I got the big lecture about not leaving anyone out, how Holi's a time to let go of grudges. Besides, I've always invited the whole class. No one wants to miss out.

Like Samantha when she was new, in the third grade. Her mother thought the Bash sounded too weird. Sam cried and cried. So her mother brought her and stayed. At first, Ms. Benson had this tight, suspicious face. By the end of the afternoon, she was tearing around the bushes, laughing, flinging powder, squirting colored water. Now she comes every year.

And the Lowells, next door. They're ancient, in their sixties. They've been coming since the Bash started, when I was three. Ms. Lowell's got a great big booming laugh and she's a wicked thrower too; she always manages to keep some extra powder hidden till the end.

I sigh happily and read over the invitation. I print the date and time in big letters. Then the bit about wearing old clothes, bringing towels and a change of clothes to go home in if they want; how we'll provide powders and colored water; and that the powders are supposed to wash out but don't always. Then about no squirt guns being allowed, because Mom and Dad can't stand guns of any sort, and then the bit about the rain date.

By the time I finish, I'm all wound up. I can hardly wait. It'll be Nanaji's first time with us for Holi, too — oh, oh!

What's that going to be like? Is he going to get in the way? I mean, he can be so fussy...

Nah. Even he can't spoil this. He loves Holi. Hey! I sort of remember him telling me something, years ago, about playing Holi when he was a kid. Something about getting back at a mean teacher.

Now that's an idea — Craig.

I grab the phone and call Jessie. "Guess what?"

"What?"

"You know, my Holi party?"

"Yeah. Just a week and a half," Jess squeals. "Can't wait."

"So how about something special for our buddy Craig? I mean, if I have to invite him…"

"Yeah! Great idea!" I can hear the grin in her voice. "What do you have in mind?"

"I don't know, like maybe save a special bottle for him? Wait 'til everything else is gone, and then get him."

Jessie says eagerly, "Yeah. And we can stash it in our secret hidey-hole."

That's what we call the hollow at the bottom of the biggest spruce tree. It's way at the far corner of the woody area of our yard. Our yard's wedge shaped and huge. About a quarter of it is woods, and kids love to duck behind the trees for Holi, but not a whole lot go right to the back.

It's perfect! Craig always grabs two spray bottles, and lurks behind the trees like he's some kind of cowboy. Only this time, we're going to be behind him. Just wait, Craig. You're in for a big surprise!

chapter three

When Mom and Dad get home I show them the invitation.

Dad pulls off his tie and drops a quick kiss on my cheek. He's got that hospital soap smell on him that always makes the insides of my nose curl.

"And what fiendish thing are you plotting this year, Mina?"

I grin and swat at him.

Mom's flying through her usual after-work routine — hanging up her blue coat in the closet, taking off her shoes and putting on her slippers, tucking her briefcase flat against the wall. She picks up her mail and scans it quickly. She looks a bit tired — she's designing a new building for some computer company and she's working flat out, even for her. But her eyes light up when I show her the invitation.

"Lovely, Mina," she smiles. She starts peeling off her jacket as she runs upstairs. "I'm going to take a quick shower. Thank goodness for your Nanaji, I don't know what we'd do without him." She turns around, halfway up. "Mina, do help out — set the table, please?"

I take out the plates and cutlery, and set the kitchen table at the bay window while Nanaji stirs the pots.

"Don't forget the pickle and yogurt, Minakshi," says Nanaji. "Wait, let me wipe that bottle. And napkins."

I sigh silently.

When we're all seated, I take a small helping of everything. There's *dahl* — a yellow lentil curry — rice, some eggplant and cauliflower. It's like Nanaji cooks the same things over and over. And no meat. We never had it that often, but now…Mom thinks it's great and we should all turn vegetarian. It kind of makes me want to run out and cram a burger in my mouth — except I never really liked them that much.

Nanaji starts, "Look how you eat. Like a little bird. How will you grow big and strong like your mummyji if you don't eat?"

Mom tucks a strand of wet hair behind her ear and eyes me warningly.

"Doctorji, look at your daughter." Nanaji calls Dad *Doctorji* whenever he talks about health.

Dad says quickly, "Don't worry, she'll grow. Like a weed. Kids always manage to." He grins at me and changes the subject to something about work.

I concentrate on finishing my food while they talk.

Okay, so I'm glad Dad got Nanaji to stop bugging me but it's just — things sure are different now. For starters, there's way more slipping and sliding from English to Hindi. And it's the three of them talking. I mean, I used to have my space — but now it's either no attention or the wrong kind.

I finish quickly and excuse myself.

Dad says, "Better get ready for the open house, kiddo. We'll have to leave soon if we want to park anywhere near your school."

I take off to my room and pull on a clean sweatshirt over my jeans. I look at myself in the mirror. Blah! Okay, so Bruce said I have gorgeous eyes, but that was last year, when he had a crush on me. Am I ever glad I never liked him back. Now he's all over Ashley like a bad rash. He just *loves* her blond hair. I never saw anyone fuss so much with hair as she does.

I swipe the brush through mine and tie it into a ponytail. It's a bit crooked, but who cares? At least my ice-pick elbows and knobby knees are covered.

When it's time to go, Nanaji comes downstairs wearing a jacket and tie. He looks all dressed up in his old-fashioned way — it's kind of cute. I get a slight whiff of his soap and aftershave, the same ones he's used forever. It reminds me of when I was little, listening to Nanaji's stories.

I whistle. "Wow, do you ever look smooth, Nanaji."

He laughs and bows slightly. "And you? You're not wearing a dress?"

My grin freezes. What does he think I am, two?

"Nanaji, everyone dresses like this."

"Hah. Everyone. All right. At least comb your hair."

I dart a look at him then turn away. "I did."

Mom says, "It's okay, Daddyji. Children these days dress more casually." She tries to straighten my ponytail but I jerk away.

She's wearing black pants and her red and blue sweater. Is that dressy enough? And Dad's jeans? How come he doesn't tell them to change?

As we climb into the car, Nanaji looks at me closely. "You look very nice, Minakshi. I didn't mean anything different."

I catch Dad's eye in the rearview mirror and mutter, "It's okay."

Dad's pretty easy-going, but boy, does he ever get mad if I'm rude to Nanaji.

Nanaji pats my hand.

I don't move.

As soon as Dad parks, I scramble out of the car. Jessie's family is just pulling in a bit ahead.

As they wave and come toward us, I grab Jess and pull her away. "Let's go, quick."

"What's up?"

I whisper, "I want to get away from my grandfather. He's kind of bugging me." I tell her about it.

She squints at me. "What're you complaining about? Hey, you've met my Grandma Henley. Your grandfather never yells — he never does the banshee. I mean, your grandfather, he's an angel compared to her, he's..."

Our parents are getting closer.

"Come on." I tug at Jessie and wave to Mom and Dad. "See you later."

Nanaji says in Hindi, "Minakshi, aren't you coming with us?"

Geez. Is he ever loud. People are looking.

Dad says something to Nanaji, then calls out, "Meet you in your class, Mina."

chapter four

The school's packed, but right in front of the gym doors we see Ashley Hughes with her parents and her brother Trevor. He's a couple of years younger than her and he's pale and sulky-looking and always sounds like he's stuffed up with a cold. Jessie's younger brother Liam is in the same class — he says no one likes Trevor much because he's always bragging about how smart he is, and about his video games.

Jessie nudges me. "Get a load of Ashley's mom."

Ms. Hughes is decked out in a green suit that's straight out of a fashion magazine, and she's perfectly made up — lips outlined and filled in, blush, layers of eye shadow — just like a model. Ashley waves and comes toward us.

"Mom, Dad, you remember Mina Salvi?" Ashley always speaks in a high, cheerleader kind of voice. "She's got to come to my birthday party this summer. For *sure*." She tosses her blond hair off her face and gives me this weird grin.

Her parents smile. Ms. Hughes smells so strongly of perfume, it's gaggy. But I like the look of her father — tall with graying, curly hair and a twinkle in his eye. He's got Ashley figured out.

"Coming up to your famous Spring Bash, huh? Your mother told me about it. Sounds terrific."

I grin back at him. I bet he'd like it. But Ms. Hughes — does she even have any old clothes?

Trevor tugs at Mr. Hughes' sleeve, "Come on, Dad, I want to show you my science project — it's the best in the class." He sniffs thickly. It's really gross.

Ashley flashes a big grin. "See you later, Mina. Save a place for me next to you in class, okay?"

As we squeeze through the crowd, Jessie whispers, "Boy, is Ashley ever being *sweet*."

We both make gagging noises, then burst out laughing.

I catch sight of Mom, Dad and Nanaji going toward our class. Nanaji looks like he's enjoying himself.

We find Terra, Noelle and Heidi, and just for fun, we stop at all the kiddy classes on the way, look at the artwork on the walls — I can't believe we ever did stuff like that.

In the second grade class we find the usual row of papier-mâché puppets — Ms. Stern's class makes them every year.

Jess shakes her head. "Kids nowadays. Murgatroyd and Blither-Dither were way better."

I grin. "Do you remember how mad Ms. Stern was when you spilled the bucket of paste?"

Jessie's eyes dance. "And how you got strips of paper stuck on the back of her atlas?"

That's when we became best friends, Jess and I, making those puppets. Mine was Murgatroyd. She had a huge hook nose and was always shouting, *"You lily-livered poltroon."* I don't know where I got that from. Jessie's was Blither-Dither. She had a mess of shocking-pink yarn hair and was always squealing, *"Och, git away you foul wee beastie!"* Jess got that straight from her Grandma Henley.

Jess and I made more puppets in her kitchen and put on shows. We even sold tickets for some of the better ones — but no one coughed up except for our parents and the Lowells next door. And Ms. Lowell laughed in all the wrong places.

By the time we get to our class it's packed. Nanaji is in the far-front corner, reading my essay up on the wall. It's on toads. I wrote it like I was the toad — how I love to eat flies and stuff. Ms. Shaw read it out loud and everyone laughed.

Mom and Dad are around the front of the class, too, by the chalkboard, talking to Ashley's and Jessie's parents. Ashley and Trevor are hanging around by themselves on the other side of Nanaji. Ashley looks bored leaning against the wall. I guess Sam isn't here yet and no one else is good enough for her.

I hear Nanaji's big, rolling laugh as he reads my essay. Ashley turns to look at him. My back stiffens.

Mom waves at me and Jessie. We start to work our way toward them, but Lina grabs Jessie to talk about the project they're doing together. I wait around a bit, then go on by myself, talking to a few kids on the way.

By the time I get near the front corner, Nanaji and Jessie's dad are deep into one of their boring conversations. Mr. Henley teaches philosophy at the university and he and Nanaji love to go on about eastern and western philosophy — how they're the same, how they're different.

It's like I hear Nanaji's voice over everyone else's. My back starts to feel itchy and squirmy.

"…it is the same journey, we are all climbing the same mountain — only we take different routes." He brings his hand down on the word same.

Mr. Henley is nodding.

Oh, no. Ashley's watching Nanaji.

I stare at Craig's drawing of a green and purple alien, but I still hear Nanaji's voice.

"…common to all humanity, the search for happiness…ancient Indian texts, the Vedas…they searched inside…not material factors…who am I, what is the purpose of life? How can I be happy, how do I find my true self…?"

I don't mean to, but my eyes turn toward Ashley.

She's staring at Nanaji. Trevor, too. My stomach feels funny — like the bottom just dropped out.

Ashley's hand comes up to her mouth. She's…she's giggling.

Thank goodness, Nanaji and Mr. Henley are finally moving out of earshot.

Ashley grins at Trevor. I want to turn away, but it's like I'm frozen, my eyes glued on Ashley.

She wags her head from side to side. "Same mountain, different routes. Ancient Indian texts. Who am I?" It's a horrible, put-on Indian accent.

There's a funny roaring in my ears.

It isn't loud enough to drown out Ashley. "Oh, yes, indeed, who am I? A stupid old geek who can't even talk right." She tosses her hair and bursts out giggling.

My Nanaji.

I feel like I'm choking.

That freaking cow — how could she?

chapter five

Jessie thumps my shoulder. "Come on. Let's get to the back."

I blink. Everything looks slightly strange.

Ashley and Trevor are still giggling.

Jessie tugs my sleeve. "Come on, Mina, what's with you?"

Then she sees where I'm looking.

She rolls her eyes and huffs, "*Now* what did she do?" She shakes my arm. "What, Mina? Tell."

My tongue's stuck to the roof of my mouth.

Jessie pulls me to the back of the class and around the corner to the storage alcove. No one's there.

"Okay, Mina, talk."

My voice comes out shaky, "They were making fun of...of my grandfather." I take a deep breath.

"The way he talks."

"You're kidding." Jessie's blue eyes flash. "What did they say?"

My chest tightens. It makes me sick to say it. "She...she called him a stupid old geek, who can't even," I choke, "talk right."

"What?" Jessie turns to look across the classroom at Ashley and Trevor.

Her face flushes until her freckles disappear. "Ashley's such a moron. And a big fat hypocrite. I mean, the way she's been buddying up to you. Let's go and tell her off."

"No!"

"Come on, she has it coming, we'll both go."

Part of me leaps at the idea, but more of me, way more, just wants to run and hide.

Jessie opens her mouth to insist, then stops, and pats my back.

"Hey, who cares what she and her dweeby brother say. Don't let her get to you, Mina — she's not worth it."

"Yeah. She's not." But my voice wobbles. Why do I feel like there's a knife in my chest?

"Hey, what's up?" It's Heidi, Terra, Noelle and a few others.

Jess swings around, her hand on her waist. "It's that snotbag, Ashley, and her creepazoid brother."

My stomach lurches. No! I don't want anyone else to know.

Jessie's eyes blaze. "They were making fun of Mr. Sharma, you know, Mina's grandfather. Imitating the way he talks. Can you imagine? Ashley called him a stupid old geek who can't even talk right."

I flinch.

"Ouch!" Terra makes a face and pushes back her red hair.

"What's her problem, anyway?" says Heidi.

My throat starts to swell again and my eyes sting. A bunch of them cluster around, saying things about Ashley, how dumb she is, how mean, stupid — never mind, never mind. But Lina and a few others just gape at me.

"Hey, what's going on?"

It's Ashley.

She pushes through, smiling. "Hi, Mina. You telling secrets? Bet you're talking about the boys you like. Tell me. I swear, I'll never..." Her voice fades.

Heidi and Terra look at me. Jessie's arm comes around my shoulder.

"Go on," she whispers fiercely.

I have to say something — they're waiting.

I come out with, "I...I heard you, Ashley Hughes."

"What?" Her voice is too innocent.

"You. And your brother." My voice cracks.

"Making fun of her grandfather," snaps Jess.

Ashley flushes. Quickly, she says, "No, I wasn't, I—" Her voice isn't a bit convincing.

"Liar!" says Jessie scornfully. "She heard everything. It's so freaking racist."

That word makes me start to shake inside.

Ashley shifts. "Hey, I was just kidding…"

Jessie glares at her. "That's kidding?"

"It's nasty," says Heidi. She understands. Last year some boys made Nazi jokes about her mother's German accent.

Ashley lifts her chin. "Yeah, well, how was I supposed to know she could hear?"

"Is that supposed to make a difference?" cries Jessie.

"Yeah, what kind of excuse is that?" says Terra.

Ashley's face is red. She licks her lips, looks quickly at the others. Then she tosses back her hair. "Okay, okay. Sor-ry." She rolls her eyes at me. "Geez, do you have to be so sensitive?"

I gasp.

"Attention please." It's Ms. Shaw, rapping the desk up front. "Would everybody please sit down so we can get started?"

Relief ripples across Ashley's face and she turns to leave.

40

The air shimmers like heat waves. Everyone's looking at me.

I choke out, "I don't ever want to speak to her again."

"Me, neither," says Heidi, loudly.

Jessie hurls after her, "Yeah, none of us want to talk to you, Ashley Hughes."

Ashley half-turns around and shrugs. "Whatever."

Samantha comes running up. "Hey, Ashley. I've been looking everywhere—" She stops when she sees our faces.

Ashley winds her arm through Sam's and starts to whisper. I catch, "...way overreacting, wa-hay."

My hands are shaking. I try to keep them still as we head to the back of the class. All us kids stand there, while our parents sit at the desks. Lina and a few others are whispering. I'm starting to feel a bit dizzy.

Ms. Shaw is talking. I don't hear a word she says. I see Nanaji, with Mom and Dad, at the front of the class. Nanaji is listening, nodding his head at times. I wish I could just disappear.

Terra is standing next to Craig and Donny. She smiles at me then whispers into Donny's ear.

"What? What?" whispers Craig. "Tell."

My insides crumple. Not Craig. He's one of the guys who made fun of Heidi's mother. The teacher

41

made him apologize, but you could tell he didn't mean it. What if he and his buddies start looking at Nanaji and...I go cold. Then what if they start looking at me...?

Ms. Shaw asks if there are any questions, and some parents put their hands up.

Craig catches my eye and comes toward me. His freckled face is serious. "Hey, Mina, Terra told me. That Ashley's a real..." He calls her a string of names.

My heart pounds, slow, thick. He's being sarcastic, I know he is — it's not like him to be sensitive or anything.

He goes on, "I'm going to tell all my guys — Ashley's toast. History. We're not going to hang out with her, okay? You remember that, huh?" He grins, showing the gap between his front teeth.

Then I get it. It's because of the party, that's all it is. I'm mad. There's no way he means it, but my knees wobble with relief anyway. If it wasn't for the Spring Bash what would he...? I make myself smile at him.

Ms. Shaw is thanking everyone for coming and the parents are starting to leave. Craig is whispering to some of the guys.

I've got to get out of here, fast. I hurry to the front of the class with Jessie, where our parents are talking. Jessie looks important, like she's dying to tell.

Mom's half-sitting on one of the front desks as she talks to Jessie's mom. She waves at me and mouths *just a minute*, then turns back.

"Here she is," says Dad.

Nanaji beams at me and says, in English, "Ah, Minakshi. Finally, I got to see your beautiful class. And I liked your essay on toads — it was very funny." He puts his hand on my back.

I jump.

Nanaji grips my shoulder. "Are you all right, Mina?"

I nod. I want to hug him, cling to him like I used to when I was little. I also want to shake his hand off me, get away from him — as far away as possible.

chapter six

In the car, going home, Nanaji says how much he liked my art projects and my writing. "And your teacher is most intelligent. Hard working and dedicated. You're very lucky."

I half-smile at him. My head feels funny — sort of spacey but headachy.

Dad looks at me in the rear-view mirror. "You okay, kiddo? You're awfully quiet."

Mom turns around.

"Yeah, I'm fine, Dad." I clear my throat. "Just a bit tired, that's all."

Nanaji smooths my hair.

Dad's voice is teasing, "Now those are words we don't hear too often, Mina. You're up to something, right? Something devious."

Why does he always try to get me going?

"Aha. It's your Holi attack list, isn't it?"

My Holi list. On my bulletin board. Ashley's name is at the bottom. No. She's not coming. Not in a million years.

"Well?" persists Dad.

Normally, Dad and I kid around, but I mutter, "Oh, leave me alone, Dad."

"Sorry, sweetie," he says. I feel his eyes on me — it's his searching, doctor look.

Nanaji rubs my back.

I lean against him, and his arm goes around me. I wish I could stay like this forever.

Nanaji whispers, "I know you're getting big-big, but would you like your nanaji to tell you a story? Maybe the one about Krishna and the water snake?"

Mom's saying to Dad, "…and Charles Hughes is being so helpful with this new project. Such a nice man. He said something about our families getting together for a barbecue."

I straighten up, away from Nanaji. I'm way too big for this. "No thanks, Nanaji. I…I've got some stuff to do."

As soon as we get home, I run up to my room. I yank the invitation list off my bulletin board. I scratch out Ashley's name, over and over again. I scratch it until the paper tears and there's a black mark on my desk.

I stare at the sheet. I'm slightly out of breath. I shove it into my bottom drawer, under a pile of papers.

When I'm ready for bed, Mom and Dad say good night. Dad touches my forehead lightly, and looks at my eyes.

"An early night," he says, briskly, patting my shoulder. "That's all you need. Don't stay up late reading, okay?"

When they're gone, Nanaji comes in.

He sits down on the edge of my bed and smiles. "Good night, Minu."

He used to call me that when I was little. He bends over to hug me.

I hug him back. My throat squeezes tight. I try to hold it in, but my eyes spill over.

Nanaji looks at me. "Tears, Minu?" His voice is soft. "What's wrong? Tell your old Nanaji."

I sniff. "Nothing. I'm...just tired."

Nanaji looks at me, in that sharp, see-everything way. Then he says gently, "Aha. Too much excitement, maybe?" He smooths my hair. "Never mind, you'll feel better after a good night's sleep, hmmm?"

The crisp smell of his soap and aftershave is like the cool night sky. When I was seven, we slept out in the courtyard of Nanaji's house because it was too hot indoors. I hated going to bed before my cousins, but Nanaji would always sit on the edge of my cot, tell me stories. About Krishna — how he was such a playful, laughing god, like a real kid, and how the kids teased him because he was dark-skinned, and how everyone loved his flute. Pretty soon, everyone would be gathered around, listening, listening. I'd lie back and watch the stars, the jasmine in Mom's hair mixing with Nanaji's aftershave, the sound of insects a chorus for Nanaji's voice.

Nanaji gives me a final hug and gets up to go. Part of me wants to call him back so badly. *Tell me a story, Nanaji, please.*

But I don't.

The door shuts behind him. I bury my face in the pillow. I try not to make any noise crying. My whole body shakes.

chapter seven

When I wake up, the sun's shining on my face through the gap in the window blinds. I blink. It can't be time to get up yet, I'm still so tired.

Then it comes rushing down like a dark cloud — yesterday evening.

I get dressed and head downstairs, slower than usual. My body feels soggy and mushy, like my head.

Nanaji is reading the newspaper while Mom bustles around in her usual clickety-clack way, making oatmeal porridge and putting together a lunch for me. Dad's already gone to work. He always leaves early.

"Mina." Nanaji smiles.

I have a hard time meeting his eyes. I go to sit down, then stop, and make myself give him a hug.

"Thank you, Minu." His voice is surprised. "Oh-ho. I don't often get hugs from my grand-daughter anymore. Feeling better this morning?"

"Yeah," I mutter. "I'm fine."

Nanaji pours me some orange juice.

He beams while I gulp it down, then goes back to the paper.

"Listen to this, Sonia," he says to Mom. He starts to read aloud from an article about new designs for communities, and how there's less crime in areas with trees, green space and walking paths. Mom's nodding — she's big on that.

I try not to listen to Nanaji's voice, try not to see it again — Ashley's hand to her mouth, gig-gling.

Was that just last night? It feels like ages ago. Or maybe a minute ago. Maybe it hasn't happened yet, maybe it won't, I wish it never…Why won't this cloudy feeling in my head clear up?

Mom dishes up the oatmeal.

I'm not very hungry.

Nanaji smiles, "Eat, eat. Oatmeal will help you grow."

I look straight down at my bowl, clench my spoon. I've got to get out of here.

At last I finish, and Jessie's at the door, waiting for me. We start walking to school.

"Hey." She thumps my arm. "How're you doing?"

I shrug.

"Did you tell your mom and dad? About what happened?"

"Of course not. Anyway, Nanaji was around."

"Oh, yeah." She smacks the side of her head then rushes on, "Well, Liam offered to pound the daylights out of Trevor." Jessie punches her fist into the air.

I half-grin. Part of me feels good that Liam wants to pound Trev, but most of me just wants to forget the whole thing.

I stop suddenly, as Jessie heads toward our usual shortcut to Lavender Drive. Ashley's house. She used to walk to school by herself, with Trevor trailing behind — until she found out about the Spring Bash.

"Come on, what's...? Oooooh!" Jessie makes a face. "You want to take the long way?"

I almost say yes. Then I clamp my jaw tight. "I'm not letting *her* change the way I go to school."

Jessie breaks into her crooked grin and slaps my back. "Way to go, Mina!"

We take the pathway and turn right on Lavender Drive toward the school. The houses are brick and humongous — some even with three car garages. I used to like this street because of the trees. Ashley's house is the one with the clump of white birches.

My hands are a bit clammy. She won't be waiting for us, she wouldn't dare.

But there they are by the gate, Ashley and Trevor. Blond hair glinting in the sunshine.

Jessie draws in a sharp breath. "I don't believe it!"

My heart starts to hammer. "We're not walking with her, are we?"

"No way," says Jessie.

As we near her front gate, we hear Ashley's voice, "Hey, what took so long, guys?" Her voice is too bright, so fake-friendly it makes me want to throw up.

Jessie and I don't say a word as we walk past. I don't even look at her, but from the corner of my eye I see her toss her hair angrily.

chapter eight

At school, we head toward our usual place by the back door, to wait for the bell. Kev, Heidi, Terra are there, as well as Nick, Josh and a few other guys. They're not too bad except when they're with Craig.

My heart beats sickeningly as we reach them. *Please, please, don't let anyone say anything.*

Terra's back is toward us, but as soon as we get there, she turns around, her red hair bouncing.

"Hey, Mina. Listen — I told my mom yesterday. She was just furious."

My heart stops. I look quickly at the other kids, wait for the flood of questions.

There's just a horrible silence. Way worse.

Then Nick clears his throat. "Yeah, Craig told us." He wriggles his nose, pushes up his glasses.

"Me and Josh, we're not talking to her."

Josh doesn't look too sure.

Heidi says, "We aren't either."

The silence feels so heavy. My face burns. What are they really thinking, the others — do they care or is it just the party? Are they maybe giggling inside? When I'm not around, are they going to make fun of...?

Suddenly, Heidi stands on her tip-toes and peers over my shoulder. "Oh my goodness — take a look at that!"

Ashley's near the clump of spruce trees by the portables. Sam's there too, and so are Kelly and Bruce and Andy. Kelly's grinning — she's always trying to hang out with Ashley. So's Bruce, of course. Normally, Ashley wouldn't even look at them.

Jessie rolls her eyes. "She's such a hypocrite."

Ashley and Sam stare in our direction. Ashley says something in Sam's ear and they burst out giggling.

Blood rushes to my face.

When the bell goes I hurry inside, ahead of the others.

In the corridor, as we take off our jackets, some of the kids whisper and look at Ashley and me. I pretend I don't notice. I make my face smile, and act like I'm totally interested in what Jessie's saying. But my head pounds and pounds.

At lunch, Jess and I make our way to the maple trees at the far end of the school yard. Most of our friends come, and a lot of the other kids, too. Okay, so it's the party, but it still feels good. Especially now.

Through all the kids running and shouting in the playground, I see Craig and the guys go by Ashley. Sam, Kelly, and a few others are with her. I'm not watching, it's not like I care or anything, but I see Ashley call out to Craig. He ignores her and comes running toward us.

Ha! Someone better get used to being with her few loser friends.

Craig gives me a blindingly-wide grin. "Hi, Mina. Hi, everyone."

"He's sure being nice," mutters Terra. "Wouldn't be worried about being invited to a party, would he?"

Some of the girls start laughing.

Craig says, "What? What?"

That just breaks them up some more. Any other time, Craig would get mad and hurl insults — he knows more bad words than anyone else — but he just grins and shrugs.

"Mina! Mina!"

It's Heidi. She's running toward us, dodging in and out of the kids in the playground.

"Guess what?" she gasps.

Jessie looks at me and makes a small face. "What, Heidi?"

Heidi puffs, "Ashley. Guess what she said about you?"

Everyone turns to me.

"Who cares?" I manage.

A lot of the kids — Craig, Lina — say, "What? What? Tell us."

Heidi takes a few huffs of breath. "Well," she says importantly. "She's going around telling everyone that you're *way* overreacting."

I try to look like I don't care.

Jessie rolls her eyes. "She's such a loser! Don't pay any attention to her, Mina."

Heidi goes on, "She said she tried to be nice to you this morning and you wouldn't look at her." She imitates Ashley's voice and bats her eyelashes, *"And I even said sorry to her yesterday. I mean, what more does she want?"*

My heart starts to race, my stomach feels sick.

Kev frowns. "She apologized? I didn't know...I mean, if she..." He squints at me. He's one of the quieter guys. I've seen how his ears go red when he looks at Ashley.

56

"She calls *that* an apology?" asks Jessie scornfully.

Some of the kids shift around and look away. They don't get it, they didn't see Ashley, giggling — what if they take her side?

I say loudly, "Who cares what she says? I've got better things to think about." My voice sounds weird even to me.

They're staring.

My insides twist with panic.

"Hey, I've got my party to plan, haven't I? Figure out who to invite."

I can't believe I actually said that. My face is so hot, like it's going to explode.

Craig asks, half shy, half eager, "When's it going to be, Mina?"

I make my mouth smile. "A week from Saturday. I'll be handing out invitations tomorrow. Or Friday."

Terra's eyes shine. "Yes!"

Craig flushes. "You inviting the whole class again?"

My head's all jumbled, muddy, my smile stuck. "Just about. All *my* friends, anyway."

Heidi pipes up, "You're not going to invite *her*, are you?"

"No way!" I know Heidi will tell Andy, because she likes him. And he's best friends with Bruce — and Bruce'll tell Ashley.

Lina and some of the others turn to look at Ashley. Lina's one of the ones who tries to dress and act like Ashley.

The words just burst out of my mouth, "Or any of *her* little friends."

This time the silence is tight, sharp, like an ax.

I hate it when kids try and get others to gang up, I never do that, and I'm not, I'm not — it's just — this is different.

Jessie thumps my back. "Yeah!"

Lina tries a smile. It's way fake.

"Good for you," says Craig. "Who needs her? Any of them?" His grin is kind of nervous.

The way they look — it makes me feel like I have a rock and I can crush a bunch of squirming little bugs. It feels awful…but also good in a sickening kind of way.

At last, Terra breaks the silence, saying something about my party last year, about how Craig got Steve's mother by mistake and how cool she was, grabbing his bottle and squirting him back. Soon, everybody's laughing and talking.

My mouth feels pinched and shaky. What am I going to do? Who do I leave out? Lina talked to Ashley this morning — does that count?

I try to follow the conversation, but I keep catching sight of Ashley's blond head. Nanaji, going on about eating right, Ashley giggling, Nanaji enjoying the open house, telling me stories, Ashley giggling, always giggling, *stupid old geek who can't even talk right.*

chapter nine

When I get home, I make myself stay in the kitchen with Nanaji while I eat my snack. I try and answer all his questions about school patiently, but I have a hard time sitting still. Finally, I escape to the study with the invitations as my excuse.

I slump in the chair, and play around with my usual computer games. I hear Nanaji bustling around the kitchen, the bang of his spoon against the pot. I try Solitaire and FreeCell until my eyes cross over. It's usually more fun.

Finally, I click on the Spring Bash file. The invitation comes up on the screen. How many should I print?

I set the printer for fifty. Ten less than last year.

I chew my lip. Every year we end up inviting more people. Mom will wonder.

I change it to seventy. If I take my usual pile, maybe Mom won't ask...

I stare at the bright, spring-like colors as the printer slides out the invitations. My head feels gray.

I shake myself angrily. I'm not going to worry — it's going to be a great party. The best ever.

Just as I finish, Mom comes into the study with her briefcase. She smiles when she sees the invitations.

"Here you are. Thanks, Mina. It's about time we got them ready." She hugs me quickly and puts her briefcase on the table by the couch.

"How many did you print?"

"Seventy."

"Perfect. You're inviting your whole class again, aren't you?"

My heart skips a beat. "Mmm," I say, crossing my toes. That can mean anything.

"Good, good," says Mom briskly. She plunks down on the couch and clicks open her briefcase. Tucking her hair behind her ear, she asks absent-mindedly, "Craig included, this year?"

"Yes, Mom." I smile my shining *good and obedient girl* smile. "For sure."

"That's the girl. Holi is about letting go of grudges — you don't want to leave anyone out." She looks up suddenly, over her glasses. "Oh, and of course, Charles Hughes' daughter — Ashley, isn't it? Don't forget her, she's new."

My head throbs.

"Mmm." I try and keep my face innocent as I head for the door. She's too tired, busy — she won't notice. Please don't let her notice.

My hand's on the doorknob when she says, "Mina?"

Oh, no.

"Come here a minute."

My heart sinks as I turn around. It's her deep look, the one I hardly ever get past.

"You are inviting Ashley, aren't you?"

I search frantically in my head for something to say.

Her eyes narrow. "What's going on?"

I clear my throat, and say in my most mature voice, "Mom, I can't invite her. You just have to trust me."

As if I didn't know that wouldn't work.

Mom takes off her glasses and puts down her papers. Oh, great.

"What happened?"

"Mom, it isn't like Craig last year, okay? It's different."

Mom pats the couch, firmly. "Come and sit down, Mina."

I sit as far away from her as I can and cross my arms.

Mom's voice is sharp. "Look Mina, you can't leave her out. Besides, she's the daughter of one of my colleagues."

"Mom, there's no way I'm having Ashley Hughes here. I'd rather eat dirt."

Mom's left eyebrow flies upwards. Here it comes, the lecture about the tone I'm using.

But instead, Mom lowers her voice. It's a trick she sometimes uses to get me to talk. Except she can't quite hide her impatience. "Mina, tell me what the problem is. Maybe we can sort it out."

"No!" I almost shout. It's not going to work this time.

"Watch your tone young lady — you may not speak to me like that." She presses her lips tightly together. "All right. If you don't want to invite Ashley, don't. But I am inviting Charles Hughes — and his whole family."

I gasp. Then it's like the dam bursts and words pour out.

"Mom, you can't invite her, you don't know what she did. It was at the open house, Mom, she and her creepy little brother, they were making fun of Nanaji. They were imitating his accent and giggling. I heard them, Mom. She..." I choke, "she called him a stupid old geek who can't even talk right, I heard her, Mom, it was so..." I stumble over the word, "ra...racist."

Mom leans forward. "What're you saying? What happened?"

My mouth shakes.

Mom pulls me into her arms, pats my back.

I gulp in deep breaths, blink hard.

Mom says tightly, "Tell me again. From the beginning."

I start over and Mom interrupts with the odd question.

She squares her jaw. "Well."

Her hands are so still on her lap, it hurts to look at her.

"*Why* do people act like that? Aren't we past this kind of crap?"

I jump. Mom hardly ever uses that kind of language.

"I'm sorry you had to go through it. It's, it's…" she searches for the right word, comes out with, "unpleasant. Hurtful."

My eyes prick again. It's awful seeing the hard line of her jaw — but at least now she won't invite Ashley.

Mom smooths my arm. "Don't keep things like that to yourself, okay, Mina? It helps to talk. Eases the hurt a little."

I nod.

"I'm glad, at least, that your friends supported you. That probably made Ashley think more than anything else." Mom's eyes are cold. "Maybe at the party Ashley will realize that it isn't accents that make people."

The bottom falls out of my stomach. "Mom! No!"

Mom says, sharply, "What good does it do to leave her out? Just because she behaved badly doesn't mean you have to."

"Mom, you didn't see her. It was so hateful, so—"

"Yes, but she apologized."

"So-o-rry?" I imitate Ashley. "That's an apology? She only said it because everyone was mad at her. She's going around saying that I'm too sensitive. She still doesn't get it, she—"

"Now calm down, Mina." Mom's face is going back to her smooth, grown-up expression. "Charles Hughes works with me, and he's one of the nicest people. I can't believe his daughter— "

As I open my mouth, she interrupts, "Not everyone who makes fun of an accent is racist. Sometimes, it's just being stupid, not thinking. Hopefully, Ashley has learned— "

"What has she learned, Mom? You should have seen her today, she— "

Mom says quickly, "Mina, there's something for you to learn from this, too." Sometimes she sounds just like Nanaji.

"Me? What— "

Mom interrupts, "It's good that you spoke up. But now you need to let go."

I clench my jaw. I can't invite her. I won't. Not after everything I said to the other kids.

"If you're angry, it hurts you more than Ashley. Put it behind you, Mina. It's what your Nanaji would say."

My heart thumps so hard, I'm breathless. "I won't forgive her. Never."

Mom says, "You know, you've been," she pauses just a fraction of a second, "impatient with your grandfather, too. You…"

Blood rushes to my face. "How did this suddenly become about me?"

"Mina, be aware of why you're doing things, be—"

Aware. The word makes me explode.

"I am aware. I'm aware of what she did. I don't need to be any more aware, Mom. I'm *not* inviting her."

Mom opens her mouth then clamps it tight.

I don't care if she's mad, I don't care if she grounds me forever.

"All right, Minakshi." Her voice is cool, hard. She only calls me Minakshi when she's way serious. "But I still plan to invite her, and that's final."

chapter ten

I toss and turn in bed until my sheets are all tangled.

For the hundredth time, I pound my pillow. Mom and Dad just don't get it. Dad — at first he tries to act all sympathetic, *I know how you feel.* But the minute he sees I'm not changing my mind he looks disappointed and trots out the usual grown-up crap — *it's the right thing to do, Mina; when you're older you'll understand.*

Jess was so mad, too, when I called her. And *what* will the other kids say?

It's not fair, it's so not fair.

Ashley at my party. Her brother, too. After everything she did — what's she going to learn from that? That you can act like a nasty pig and still get invited to parties? Where's the justice?

Ashley laughing, dodging, throwing powders…it's supposed to be a fabulous time, wild, brilliant colors.

Suddenly, my stomach jolts upside down. Nanaji. He'll be there. What if Ashley starts looking, giggling — what if she gets the other kids…?

I go cold.

They wouldn't dare, would they? But Ashley, she could be laughing inside, and then, after the party…

I stare at the ceiling, at my mobile of the solar system, the glow-in-the-dark stars I stuck on last year. They don't seem that bright anymore.

I curl my knees up and hug them close. It takes a long time to stop shivering.

I'm exhausted. I lie very still.

That's when it comes to me.

Of course.

Why didn't I think of it before?

Mom and Dad *can't* just make me invite someone I hate to my party. Ashley *can't* just laugh at people, can't just…

Yes, it's perfect.

I have to do it.

For Nanaji.

In the morning, before breakfast, I head to Mom's room. I'd better get it over with now, when she's busy. Dad's already gone to work, Nanaji will be in his room, probably sitting for meditation.

Mom's at her dressing table, screwing on the backs of her pearl earrings.

Her eyes meet mine in the mirror.

I clear my throat. "I've been thinking about it. And...and I've decided to invite Ashley after all."

Mom's face relaxes. "I'm so glad, Mina. I was hoping you'd come around — it really is better this way." She turns to look at me, then drops the back of her earring. "Oops!"

By the time I find it, she's glancing at her watch. Lucky for me.

Jessie has early soccer practice so I walk to school alone.

I don't bother with the short-cut to Lavender Drive, but take the long way around. It's not that I'm chicken, it's just — I've got enough to deal with.

As we wait for the school doors to open, Ashley's way over by the far portable — with her new friends. I keep a lookout for Jess, but the bell goes and we're all heading into class before she comes tearing in. Her jacket flaps, her hair's all wild and her face is glowing from soccer.

I mouth at her, *I'll tell you later*, but I don't think she gets it.

I unzip my bag and take out the invitations. Heidi and a few others start to whisper, grin. You can feel the wave of excitement wash through the class. Kelly smiles shakily at me. Her sandy eyelashes blink, up and down, up and down.

My heart skips a beat. What are the kids going to think — especially after everything I said yesterday?

I start with my row, and give each kid an invitation. Ashley and Sam are at the opposite end of the classroom. Ashley's eyes are glued to her book — she's pretending not to notice.

When I give Kelly one, she looks up, shocked. She chokes out, "Thanks, Mina."

Okay, so a small bit of me is relieved I don't have to leave her out, but I'm mad too. Especially at the way Lina turns to look quickly at Ashley, like she's so worried about her.

I get to the last row. I keep my smile pasted on and move along steadily. Sam's head jerks like a yo-yo when I put an invitation on her desk.

Ashley is next.

I pause. I'd so like to skip her.

But I slap one down on her desk, too.

"What's this?" she asks shrilly, like she doesn't know.

I don't bother to look at her. *You just wait, Ashley Hughes.*

There's a buzz as kids read the invitations. Some look at me and Ashley, nudge each other and whisper. Heidi's mouth is half open.

My ears are burning by the time I get back to my desk.

Jessie leans over and hisses, "Are you nuts? Why…"

Ms. Shaw asks us all to stand for the National Anthem.

I whisper, "Tell you later."

There's no chance to talk in class — Ms. Shaw is really fussy about what she calls extraneous chatter, and I can't tell Jessie in a note.

I know she's having a hard time listening to Ms. Shaw. She fidgets, shifts, looks at me. A few times she thumps down her pencil, sighs heavily.

At last, the bell goes for recess. Jessie pulls me outside to the far end of the yard.

"Okay, Mina. Talk. Fast. Before the others get here." She puts her hand on her hip. "I thought you weren't going to invite Ashley, whatever your Mom and Dad said."

"I wasn't. But now I want her to come." I smile — a tough, *I'm just doing what I gotta do* smile.

Jessie squints at me. "Are you totally crazy?"

I roll my eyes slightly. "Think about it Jess. It's Holi."

"Huh?"

"If she's right there, in my yard, and we're throwing around powders…"

Slowly, light dawns in her eyes. "Ohhhhh!"

"Yup!" I pound my right fist into my left palm. "I'm going to get her."

Jessie whoops and give me a high five.

"And the best part is, Mom can't do a thing about it."

Jessie grabs my arm. "So what're we doing?"

"Don't know yet — but it has to be big, Jess. Stupendous. Something to make her learn she can't get away with—"

Jessie's eyes gleam. "Yeah!"

"You in?"

"Try and stop me!" Her freckles dance.

For the first time all morning, my neck loosens. My stomach tingles with excitement. Jess is the best friend in the world. I hug her.

Jessie says quickly, "Shh. Here come the others. Not a word — we don't want it getting back to her."

Heidi, Terra, and a few others — even guys — come running up to us.

Terra blurts, "Mina, what are you doing? Why did you invite Ashley?"

"Yeah?" squeaks Heidi.

My face goes hot. Jessie nudges me warningly.

I roll my eyes. "My mother made me." Well, it's true, too.

Terra makes a sympathetic face.

Heidi says, "I kinda figured it was something like that." She looks sideways at Craig. She knows what happened last year.

Craig snorts, "Parents." Then his eyes brighten and he flashes his gappy smile at me. "Hey, Mina, if she's coming to your party, do you want me to get her for you?"

My eyes fly to Jessie. There's no one like Craig for thinking up revenge. Maybe…

Jessie looks sideways at Nick and Lina and shakes her head slightly. Nick lives next door to Bruce. And Lina, who knows? Besides, I want to get Ashley myself — it has to be me.

I swallow hard and say so prissily it almost makes me gag, "Forget it, Craig. My mother would freak out — you know what she's like."

Craig's face falls.

Quickly, Jessie has us all laughing and talking about last year's party. Craig's the loudest.

Recess is almost over when Ashley, Sam and a few others walk by.

Ashley acts surprised to see us. "Oh, hi, Mina." Her voice is high with fake-friendliness.

I can't breathe.

Jessie hisses in my ear, "You want her to come, don't you?"

I jerk out, "Hi, Ashley."

Ashley hesitates, then casually comes closer.

I clench my jaw. Lina's smiling her head off at Ashley.

Ashley starts talking about a new jacket she bought, and how she found this great shampoo from Australia that's just so perfect for her hair. She doesn't look a whole lot at me.

Jessie winks.

I smile. *It's not over yet, Ashley.*

chapter eleven

Saturday afternoon, Jess and I hang out in my room, and throw around ideas for *Operation Get Ashley*.

But we can't come up with anything that satisfies me. Soaking Ashley with the hose, tossing ice down her shirt, throwing food at her — none of it's good enough. It has to be something so she'll think twice about making fun...so everyone will laugh at *her*. So she'll never forget.

Jessie's ideas get wilder and wilder. "Stink bombs," she says desperately. "Rotten eggs? Okay, okay, I know. It has to be something that won't ruin the party. Or get us into serious trouble. Aaargh!" She pulls her hair wildly and flops on my bed. "Why can't we save a bottle 'til the end, like we talked about for Craig? What's with you? You're so..."

"What?"

Jessie sits up and grins. "Mad. Tight."

"Yeah, well, it has to be something that fits the crime, doesn't it? We're not just going to do some kiddy stuff — it has to be really good."

Jessie rolls her eyes slightly.

I blink hard. "Okay, if you don't want to, I'll do it myself."

Jessie thumps me with the pillow. *"Och, git away, you foul wee beastie."* We break into a pillow fight.

But we don't have a single good idea by the time Jessie has to go home.

I pace up and down, scuffing my toes against the blue carpet. I flop on my bed and try and kick up at my mobile — I nearly knock off Jupiter. I sit at my desk by the window, stare at my roller-coaster game, color in one more square green. My latest card is face up: *Your roller-coaster car goes off track. You plunge to your death.* Jess and I were going to make up more cards, only *Operation Get Ashley* is way more important.

But I still haven't thought of anything when Mom calls me to dinner.

I sniff as I go into the kitchen. Something smells good.

Mom's humming softly, wearing her comfy Saturday clothes — a soft-blue and yellow *salvar khameez*, baggy Indian pants and tunic. Her hair is loose. When she sees me, she smiles in a funny way.

Hey, she cooked today! It's my favorite — ravioli with her homemade tomato sauce. A peace offering.

I'm still kind of mad at her, but I take a huge helping anyway.

"Delicious, Sonia," says Nanaji. His eyes twinkle when he sees my plate. "Ha. Your old Nanaji is going to have to learn to cook things like this. The plain Indian food gets boring, no?"

"No, really," I say politely. "It's fine."

Nanaji smiles. "You don't have to be so formal with me, Minu." He turns to Dad and Mom. "What nice-nice manners she has."

Dad winks. "Oh, she has her moments."

I grin and work my way through the ravioli. I don't pay much attention to their conversation, I mean, some of it's in Hindi and I can't be bothered concentrating. Besides, I still have to figure out how to get Ashley.

Dad interrupts my thoughts. "What're you up to, Mina? I can see the wheels turning. It always worries me when you're this quiet."

I put down my fork and half-grin, guiltily. "Give me a break, Dad."

Nanaji chuckles. "With Holi coming up, she's got a right to some secrets." He smiles at me. "Oh-ho, I remember some awful things I did."

My ears prick up. I lean forward eagerly. "What, Nanaji? Tell."

Nanaji shakes his head. "No, no, I don't want to give you ideas."

"Nanaji! Come on. Anyway, I'm old enough to know what to do and what not to do — even if you didn't."

Nanaji bursts out laughing. I feel warm and easy — it's like we're comfortable together, just like we used to be.

"Smart girl, my Minakshi," says Nanaji. He squeezes my hand and I squeeze back.

"So, what did you do?"

Dad says, "You'll have to tell now, Daddyji. Mina won't let up until you do — she can be more tenacious than a bulldog."

Mom shakes her head. But she's smiling, too.

Nanaji settles back in his chair. "Well, now, I remember Mr. Motilal. He taught us Geography. Oh-ho, he was a strict-strict teacher. Not nice and kind like your teachers. If we so much as spoke one word out of turn, we'd get it, *phutta-phut*, a smack on the arm. So Ravi, my best friend, and I, we got a special color mixed for him. We threw in all-all different colors — it was so messy, so dirty, I can't tell you." Nanaji chuckles. "Now you don't do this, okay?" He looks warningly at me. "Promise?"

I smile, cross my toes.

Nanaji goes on. "We mixed into it some old, stale cooking oil my mother was going to throw out."

Mom drops her face on her hand and groans, "Oh, no."

Dad laughs.

"With the oil, the colors don't wash. You should have seen the poor man. We got his face, his shirt, his hair. He had white hair and it looked so awful — that dirty color — it was like mud, worse than mud. He had to scrub and scrub. And the shirt, it never washed clean. It was lucky his hair didn't stain too, poor man."

It's like electricity crawling up my back. Nanaji's always going on about karma. It's supposed to be the law of cause and effect — how everything you do results in something.

It fits. Ashley makes fun of Nanaji. Nanaji gives me a clue about how to get her back.

An ugly, dirty color. That'll take the cool right out of her. I can just see it — all of us in bright colors and Ashley splashed with something really yucky. All over

79

her shirt, her arms, her *hair*. Yes! Her precious hair. *With something that will stain.*

I kind of hear Nanaji saying something about how he felt bad afterwards, how the teacher took it so well, something about not holding grudges, but I'm hardly listening.

I'm thinking about Kevin's brother, Luke.

Mom's voice breaks my thoughts. "Mina."

I jerk up and look at her.

Mom wags her finger. "You are not to do anything with oil — I want to make that *quite* clear."

Dad and Nanaji stop talking.

Nanaji says, "No oil, Mina. You must not. I was so little when I did that, and it wasn't kind...I should never have done it."

Dad's eyes are half-laughing, half-watching.

I smile. "Of course I won't."

Mom's face is still suspicious.

"What?" My voice squeaks innocently. "I promise. No oil."

Mom relaxes.

Nanaji says, soothingly, "Of course she won't. She's smart enough to know better." He smiles. "Now, Sonia, remember some of the things you got up to..."

Mom flushes, laughs. She quickly changes the subject and they start talking about one of Mom's old neighbors in a mixture of Hindi and English.

I keep my face calm, but inside, I'm jumping about. She didn't make me promise not to mix a yucky color — she was just worried about the oil.

Who needs oil, anyway? Not me. No way. I know *exactly* how to get Ashley's hair, without any greasy, old oil — yeah, I am smart enough for that.

Luke — Kev's brother. He dyed his hair purple with drink crystals. *That's* what we'll use. Only it's not going to be any nice color like purple, it's going to be a mixture — a sickly, yucky mess.

My head buzzes. The stuff is cheap, so even with the money I've got I'll be able to get enough, and mix it up extra strong. Luke complained that it didn't last long, but even a few days would be awesome. Just long enough so Ashley'll have to show up in school like that — so everyone will laugh and laugh.

Something shakes inside me. Am I going too far?

I lick my lips nervously and look at Nanaji.

His eyes shine as he talks. They're brown, but faded with that light bit around the edge that old people have. He sees me looking at him and smiles.

My throat goes funny.

No. I have to do it. For him. For my nanaji who came to the open house, all spruced up, eager.

81

Ashley has to learn...it's about *justice*, that's what it is.

Anyway, it's karma, isn't it — cause and effect?

Why else would the ideas come, just when I need them?

chapter twelve

I tell Jess Sunday afternoon, when we're up in my room.

"Wow!" She thumps my arm admiringly. "Imagine you coming up with that! Hey, I didn't know you could be so bad, Mina. Where did the good little girl go?"

I grin at her. Okay, so I know I'm not *bad* like some kids — and I don't really want to be. But it feels kind of great, for once, not to be a goody-goody.

Jessie's eyes gleam. "Hey, let's put oil in, too."

"We don't need to, Jess. It's going to stain fine without oil. Anyway, I promised I wouldn't." I kind of hate to sound like a wuss, especially after being almost cool.

Jessie looks a bit disappointed, but she shrugs. "Okay. But we've got to plan it all out — like we're on a secret mission."

She hugs me and we laugh out loud.

We count my money and work out the details. I can't believe how much there is to get right. We decide we'll go to the grocery store after school on Monday — there'll be fewer questions asked that way.

Monday, Jess and I rush along Lavender Drive to school, but, thank goodness, Ashley isn't waiting. As we hang around for the doors to open, everyone's talking about the party — about last year, what the weather's going to be like, who's going to get who.

Halfway through, it hits me — not one kid mentions Ashley or the open house. And okay, I don't want them to but — it's like everyone's forgotten what she did.

I try and keep away from Ashley, but it's tough during recess. The whole class is hanging together, talking about the party, so she's there, too — sort of at the edge of the group, but still. It makes me sick. Everyone's speaking to her again. The only good thing is hardly anyone joins in when she tries to turn the conversation to her shopping — we'd all rather talk about the Bash.

After school, Jessie and I run out fast. I don't think Ashley wants to walk with us, but we're not taking any chances.

Jess goes home to tell her mother she's coming to my house and to get her money.

"Hi, Nanaji," I call out, as I open my front door. Something smells good.

I drop my bag and go into the kitchen. "What're you cooking?"

"Take a look." Nanaji smiles.

I lift the lid off the pot. Spaghetti sauce.

I grin at him.

"I made it for you, Minu. From your mother's recipe." He pinches my cheek gently.

Then Jess is at the door.

"Hi, Mr. Sharma."

"Hello, Jessie. How are you?" Nanaji always speaks English around people who don't understand Hindi because he doesn't want them to feel left out. He's big on courtesy. "Come on, sit down. Let me get you a snack."

"We're not hungry, Nanaji. Anyway, Jess and I have something to do. We'll be back soon." I turn away quickly.

"Where are you going?"

I groan silently. It sounded so easy when Jess and I were planning it.

"Oh, just..." I fumble around and come up with, "just to the grocery store."

Nanaji's eyes twinkle. "You're not buying junk food, are you?" He shakes his head. "Oh-ho. You know what your mummyji says about that. You'll get me into a pile of trouble."

"No junk food, Nanaji. I promise. It's just a...a project we're doing." There. That's not lying.

Nanaji looks at me sharply, then smiles. "I'll go with you. Your mummyji said we're low on Parmesan cheese." He turns the burner off under the pot.

"We'll get it for you," I say, quickly. "Save you the trouble."

"No trouble. You know I love to walk. Just wait, I'll get my wallet." He heads upstairs to his room.

I turn in panic to Jess. "Now what? Do we try and talk him out of coming?"

Jess presses her hands against her face. "I don't know. Yes. No. *No*. It'll just make him suspicious. We'll have to wing it."

As Nanaji comes downstairs, wearing his cardigan, I grab my old backpack from the closet. It'll come in handy to hide the stuff. I hope my pocket doesn't bulge too much with my change purse.

"Such a beautiful day," says Nanaji. "It's nice for me to have company. I walk a lot, but not often with my granddaughter, let alone you, Jessie."

My face goes hot. He sometimes asks if I want to go with him on his walks. I usually find an excuse not to.

As we take the footpath through the green space behind our street, Nanaji asks Jessie and me about school.

I feel a bit restless and itchy, but Jess starts telling him about the supply teacher, Mr. Blisten, and how he's always yelling. After a bit, I join in, too. We imitate Mr. Blisten, say how we all hate him.

Nanaji says something about not holding onto grudges. He rolls his r's. A few teenage kids pass by us. Are they looking? I walk faster.

At last, we're at the grocery store. It's busy. Good.

"We'll meet you at the exit, Nanaji," I say quickly.

"Let's meet at the check-out," he says. "I'll get whatever you and Jessie want, Minu." His eyes are warm and loving.

I flush. "Thanks, Nanaji, but it's okay." Before he can speak again, I pull Jessie away.

"See you later, Mr. Sharma," calls Jessie. She turns to me, "I like your grandfather, he's sweet."

"Yeah, well…" I mean, it's easy for her — she doesn't have to live with him, or put up with the fussing.

I say quickly, "Come on." I start to run down an aisle. "Where're the freaking drink crystals?"

Jess grabs my arm, "Hey, slow down. Read the signs."

We go down the ends of the aisles. At last, one says *Baked Goods, Drink Crystals, Beverages.*

"That's it," cries Jess.

There's a large man with a grocery cart dawdling down the aisle like he's got all day. Jessie and I dodge past him and stop, breathless, in front of the drink crystals.

I let out a whoop. "Hey, look. It's cheap, way cheap. We'll be able to get..." I have a bit over five dollars. "Fifteen!" It's a snap to figure out, especially after Nanaji's math game.

I start to grab a whole bunch — orange, green, purple, blue, red, a few other weird shades. I take two of most colors and one of the rest.

"Come on, the check-out, quick."

As we dash up the aisle, Jess stops suddenly in front of the baking supplies.

"Jessie, let's go," I huff.

Quickly, Jess picks up a package with four bottles of food coloring. Her eyes dance. "My contribution."

"But— " I start.

"Hey, come on, Mina — we're not doing the oil. At least—"

"Okay, okay!" Then we're tearing to the check-out. There isn't a single one free.

My eyes dart around frantically. Should we go for the express line even though we have more than eight items?

At the far end, I notice her — the sour-faced cashier. There's just one shopper at her cash.

I run toward her. Nanaji won't come here — one time I was with him, he tried to talk to her, but she was all surly.

Hurry, hurry, I say silently, as she passes a packet of spaghetti in front of the scanner. She weighs some broccoli. She's taking forever. I glance around. No sign of Nanaji.

Jessie keeps looking over her shoulder, too. The cashier scowls suspiciously. I nudge Jess.

At last, the woman ahead of us is through.

The cashier's name tag says Molly. Right, Jolly-Molly. She nods unsmilingly and starts to pass the packages in front of the scanner, one by one. Why can't she just scan one and count the rest? Then she scans the food coloring.

Quickly, Jess and I count out our money — all in change — and hand it to her.

"Uh-oh, he's coming," whispers Jessie. "To this check-out."

Molly's taking forever re-counting the money, like we're trying to cheat her or something. *Come on,* I scream in my head.

She puts the coins in the cash drawer, each in the right compartment, and finally reaches for a bag.

Just as Nanaji comes up, she slips our things into the bag.

Nanaji says, "Here you are, girls. I was looking for you." He eyes the grocery bag.

I stuff it into my backpack, heart racing. Did he see? Will he say anything? What if he says something in front of Mom or Dad?

I zip the bag closed, start to blab, "What did you get, Nanaji?"

"Cheese. A few other things. Hello, Molly," he smiles. "How's your cold today?"

"Hi, Mr. Sharma." The cashier's sour face actually melts into a smile. "It's much better, thank you. How are you?"

It's like she's a different person! Nanaji must come here when I'm at school...funny, I never thought about what Nanaji does during the day.

Nanaji pays for his things and says goodbye. "Now take care of yourself, Molly."

"I will, Mr. Sharma. You, too."

I look at Nanaji. How did he get her to be so human?

"Well," says Nanaji as we head home through the park, "What did you get?"

"Oh, nothing much, Nanaji."

"It's a secret," adds Jessie, grinning her head off. "A surprise."

I make a face at her to shut up behind Nanaji's back.

"Oh-ho. A secret and a surprise." He scratches his head. "And Holi coming up."

Jessie and I look at each other.

I say quickly, "Nanaji, please don't say anything to Mom or Dad, okay? Please?"

"Yeah, please, Mr. Sharma?" Jessie turns her big blue eyes pleadingly up at Nanaji, smiles her widest.

Nanaji looks at us sharply. For a minute he reminds me of Mom, when she sees right through me.

Then he chuckles and says gently, "I know nothing."

Jessie digs me with her elbow and gives me a thumbs up sign.

Nanaji is humming softly as he walks beside me, some Hindi song he used to sing when I was little.

Something funny twists inside me.

For him — I'm doing this all for him.

chapter thirteen

I have a hard time paying attention in class on Tuesday. Jess and I are going to mix the crystals after school — we figure it's best to get it out of the way before Mom gets us mixing the official powders on Friday.

I go over my mental list again — drink crystals and food coloring, safe in my bottom drawer. I sneaked a squirt bottle from the garage, and even a jug to mix the stuff in. That's it, isn't it? Why do I feel like I've forgotten something?

At recess, everyone's laughing and talking about the party. Ashley tosses the hair off her face and says, like we've all been wondering and worrying, "Yeah, my weekend's free, so I'll be able to come."

Jessie turns red and opens her mouth, but I give her a nudge and she shuts up.

Just wait, Ashley, just you wait.

Finally, school's over and Jess and I rush home. We grab a quick snack, while Nanaji asks about our day, then race up to my room.

At last. My hands tingle as I open my bottom drawer.

Jessie's pink with excitement. "Woo-hoo!" She grabs a few packages and throws them in the air.

"Hey, quit clowning, Jess. What if the packages burst on my carpet?"

"Okay, okay." Jess picks them up, and says breathlessly, "Come on, let's get mixing."

"Calm down, Jess. We have to be really careful. Remember Kev said what a mess it made — how his parents were furious at Luke?"

"All right, all right." Jess makes a face. "So where are we going to mix it?"

Good. Now she's serious. "In the main bathroom — Mom and Dad have their own. But I share with Nanaji, so we have to clean it properly."

"Then all we have to do is hide the stuff — in our hidey-hole."

"Yeah. Saturday morning. And make sure Ashley comes to the back of the woods."

Jessie's eyes dance. "And we've even got *that* figured out. Are we great or what?"

I wave the squirt bottle at Jessie and take out the jug from under my desk. "Ready?"

Jessie nods eagerly.

My heart beats faster as we creak open the door. Nanaji's downstairs. The radio's on in the family room.

"One, two, three!" We sprint for the bathroom and lock the door behind us.

We're giggling and out of breath.

"Shh," I say. "We don't want my grandfather coming up. Now, how do we mix this?"

Jessie reads the instructions. "Wow, you're supposed to put eight cups of water into one of these packages." Her eyes dance. "So, if we put in a few cups of water and *fifteen* packets, it should be really strong."

I grin at her. This is so great.

I tear the top off the first package. "Ta-dah!" I say as I pour the crystals into the jug.

"Blue, fantastical blue," sings Jess.

"Not for long," I say, opening the other packages, pouring in the crystals. Blue, green, purple, red, orange.

"Oh, man, this is going to be so sickitating!" squeals Jess.

"Does it ever smell gross. *Blech!*" I accidentally drop an empty package on the floor. "Hey, get that, Jess."

Jess goes to throw it in the garbage, then stops. She puts the empty packages back in the grocery bag. "I'll throw this in the trash can in the park — don't want anyone noticing it here." She looks awfully pleased with herself.

"Now you're thinking," I grin.

When all the crystals are finally in the jug, I turn on the tap and add some water. I want enough to make a good batch, but still really strong.

The crystals soak it up, and the mixture in the jug turns into an ugly reddish-brown.

Jessie peers at the jug. "Whoa, enough water, enough, enough."

"But we want the crystals to dissolve."

"Okay, so give me the spoon."

I turn and look at her. "Oh, no!"

"Now what?" huffs Jessie.

"I forgot," I wail. "I guess I'm going to have to go downstairs and get it."

Jess rolls her eyes. "What about your grandfather? What if he...? Oh, never mind, go, just go. Hurry."

I unlock the bathroom door and peer out. I can still hear the radio. Please let Nanaji be in the family room.

I dart silently downstairs, into the kitchen. Thank goodness, it's empty. From the jug by the stove, I grab the nearest wooden spoon. I'm halfway up the stairs before I see it's Mom's favorite. Too bad, I'm not going down again.

Jess opens the door and we laugh, me between gasps.

She grabs the spoon from me and starts to stir. Slowly, slowly, the crystals dissolve.

Jessie holds up the package of food coloring. "And now, to make it even better...!"

"Yeah, put it in, all of it!"

Jess squeezes the four bottles of coloring, one by one. As I stir, a few drops splash in the sink, making a dark stain. But the liquid in the jug is perfect — it's disgusting, like no color in the world — the most sick-making dark browny-greeny guck!

I grin widely at Jess.

"Awesome!" she breathes.

I start to pour it slowly into my old window-cleaner bottle. Some spills on my hands and on the counter.

When the squirt bottle is half full, Jessie puts her hand on my elbow, "Hey, enough. Leave some for me."

I put the jug down and turn to look at her.

"What? Didn't you get me a bottle?" Jess puts her hand on her hip. "Way to go, smartie."

"I'm sorry, I'm sorry. I could only sneak one bottle under my shirt."

"Great. What am I supposed to do?" Jess lets out a huff of breath.

"I'll get another one from the garage."

"Yeah, right. Not looking like that, you won't."

My hands are covered in the muddy color.

Jessie clicks her tongue. "There's no way I'm poking around your garage — what if your grandfather sees me?"

I bite my lip. "Okay, okay, look under the sink."

Jessie digs around, and brings out a bottle of window cleaner, about two-thirds full.

"Whaddya think?"

"Go for it. Empty it."

Jess grins.

"My mom won't notice," I say, more confidently than I feel. I rinse the bottle and nozzle well, then pour in the rest of the liquid.

"There. Done." I wipe my forehead with my sleeve. I'm hot and sweaty. There's a huge mess on the counter and in the sink, and my hands are covered in the greeny-muddy guck.

"Okay." I clear my throat. "Now we have to make sure they squirt." A beautiful spray comes out. "Yes!"

Jess picks up her bottle and sprays, too. It goes on my arm.

"Hey, watch it."

"Sorry," grins Jess. She waves her bottle around and goes to squeeze again.

"Cut it out! If we get the wall, we're done for."

"Okay, okay. Wow! Does this stuff ever stink. Like rotten fruit salad. Hey, you'd better wash up, Mina."

I look at her. "It should come off, shouldn't it? While it's fresh?"

Jess makes a face. "Sure it will."

I turn on the tap, leaving a dirty stain on it. Jessie gets the cloth from under the sink and the cream cleanser. I rinse out the jug. Luckily, it comes clean. The sink is disgusting, but the dirt comes off easily, even though the cloth turns muddy.

I start to scrub my hands with soap.

"It's not coming off," says Jessie, shakily.

I scrub harder. My heart starts to pound. I look up at Jess. "It works."

Jessie's eyes are wide. "Maybe a bit too well."

"It has to come off," I say. "It's only been on a few minutes."

The stains are worst on my palms, in the creases between my fingers and around my fingernails. I reach for the nail-brush, and scrub.

"Ouch! Good thing you didn't get any on you, Jess — your skin's way pale — it would really show up."

"Yeah." Then her face brightens. "Think how it's going to look on her hair — if it's this hard to scrub off after a few minutes, what'll it be like after a while!"

I grin and scrub harder.

Slowly, slowly, the stains come off.

At last, I give my hands a final rinse. "There, if I scrub anymore, it'll take my skin right off." There's just a faint smear in the fold between my thumb and first finger. I hope no one will notice.

"The spoon," hisses Jessie.

We both scrub it, but some of the stains won't budge — especially where the blue food coloring squirted on the handle.

"What'll I do? It's Mom's favorite."

The doorknob rattles. "Mina? You in there?"

Jessie claps her hand to her mouth. Her face is half-scared, half-laughing.

"Yeah, Nanaji, I'll just be a minute. Why don't you use the downstairs powder room?"

"I need my pills from the medicine cabinet."

"I'll be out soon, Nanaji. Go on down, I'll bring them to you when I'm done."

"No, I'll wait." Nanaji doesn't like stairs.

Jessie turns to me, eyes wide with panic.

I fumble under the sink. I find an old make-up bag. It's not quite big enough, but I shove in the jug, the squirt bottles, the soiled cloth and the spoon. The bag doesn't close — the jug and spoon stick out. Jessie turns the spoon around so the dirty end is hidden, then reaches for my towel and throws it over my arm. She scrunches the garbage bag in her hand.

"Ready?" I mouth.

She nods, wipes away her smile. Her face goes back to her usual innocent expression. It's the wide blue eyes — it fools new teachers every time.

I open the door.

Nanaji is pacing up and down.

"Ahh," he smiles. "All done?" He looks a bit surprised that Jess is there too, then glances at the bulge under the towel.

I turn sideways so my body blocks it.

I lick my lips. "Yeah, Jess and I, we were just looking for something."

As he heads for the bathroom, I take one last look.

My heart leaps into my throat. A dark blotch. Behind the sink.

Nanaji's rooting around in the medicine cabinet.

He sniffs slightly. He turns around, sees me watching. "What's the matter, Mina?"

"Nothing." I pull Jessie to my room, and tell her about the blotch.

"He'll never notice," whispers Jessie. "My dad never notices dirt."

"You don't know my grandfather," I groan. "He's way tidy."

At last, we hear Nanaji's footsteps going down. We dart back to the bathroom, and scrub the blotch off.

"D'you think he saw?" asks Jessie.

"Nah," I say. I don't feel too sure, though.

Back in my room, we hide the bottles and spoon at the back of my closet. I tuck them behind a basket of stuffed toys and puppets. Murgatroyd's hook nose sticks out from under a tiger.

"Hey," cries Jessie, grabbing the puppet. "Remember, *lily-livered poltroon*?"

We burst out laughing and flop on the floor, exhausted. My stomach is weak with laughter and excitement.

Jessie waves Murgatroyd. "Saturday. Only four more days."

I grin at her. I just love, love, love Holi. It's the best.

Then slowly, like through a fog, it comes back.

My stomach goes tight. In all the fun of mixing the crystals, getting at Ashley, I'd almost forgotten what it's all about — almost forgotten Nanaji and the open house.

How could I?

chapter fourteen

Wednesday, Thursday just crawl by. I've never had days go so slowly. Everyone in my class is talking about the party. Even Ashley's stopped pretending to be cool, and is getting excited. I can't keep totally away from her, but I'm so surrounded by kids laughing about the party, worrying about the weather, that it doesn't bother me much. I mean, everyone's falling over themselves to be nice to me. Jess and I are having the best time.

On Friday, we're all wound up so tight, Ms. Shaw gets really annoyed. "If you don't settle down, there's going to be detention for the whole class."

That makes us a bit quieter for the rest of the day.

At last, the bell rings. There's shouting and yelling as kids call out, "See you tomorrow, Mina."

Craig's grinning from ear to ear. "See ya later!" He thumps my arm and winks at me.

Jessie and I head out into the sunshine. It's warm, perfect for Holi. Heidi said it's going to be even hotter over the weekend and she should know — her father is the weatherman at the local TV station.

We turn the corner to Lavender Drive.

Jess says, "What's with Craig, anyway? The way he looked at you? Wonder what he's—"

"Mina, Jess, wait for me." Footsteps running after us.

We swing around.

Ashley.

Jessie and I make faces at each other. We haven't walked with her all week. I mean, it's a beautiful day — why did she have to go spoil it?

Ashley comes running toward us, her hair shining in the sun.

For a split second, it's like I see her for the first time. Blond hair, designer jeans and Gap shirt. Her face is happy, like she hasn't got a care in the world.

A shock wave washes through me. She's real — not just some idea in my head.

Ashley catches up, jabbering away.

My head's messy, confused. What am I doing? How can I — what's the matter with me? I was so sure...

Ashley says importantly, "My dad says we're going to bring some powders, too. I'm going to have lots and lots."

Jessie rolls her eyes at me. Okay, so Ashley's a show-off and a spoiled brat, but is that enough to...?

Ashley is talking about Bruce. On and on. Her voice buzzes like a mosquito. "He's such a pain, the way he follows me around." She clicks her tongue and tosses back her hair. "I mean, can you imagine, he even asked me out. Like I'd ever go out with him. Stupid geek!" She bursts out giggling.

Stupid old geek.

My stomach feels like it's been punched.

Ashley smiles widely as she turns up her driveway. "Bye, Mina; bye, Jess. See you tomorrow." Her brown eyes are shining, happy.

She's totally forgotten, *totally.*

My head pounds and pounds. How could I have actually started to doubt? The way she...*how* could I let Nanaji down so badly?

"Doesn't she make you sick?" whispers Jessie. She grins at me. "Wait 'til tomorrow. We're going to get her good."

It's like her voice comes from far away. I'm back at the open house, Nanaji, eyes shining, Ashley, giggling — I make myself bring it back, back, blazing hot, until I feel it again, that stab in the heart.

Jessie's blathering on about the party — something about Craig. I don't really hear her.

She digs me with her elbow. "Hey, what's the matter?"

"Nothing." I smile shakily.

She stares at me. "Something wrong with you?"

"No, nothing's wrong. Everything's fine."

It's like she's forgotten, too.

Luckily, we're just at my driveway, and I shout, "See you later to mix up the colors, okay?" I run inside.

Mom's home early. Nanaji asks me about my day. It's hard for me to look at him. I rush upstairs.

In my room, I go over the open house again and again, what happened — I've got to keep it clear, remember why I'm doing this. I won't let Nanaji down again.

Mom calls me to dinner.

When I go into the kitchen, Nanaji smiles. "You went up so fast-fast, Minu. Are you all right?"

"Yeah, of course. I'm fine, Nanaji."

Nanaji looks at me for a long time. He puts his hand gently on my shoulder and squeezes.

He did the same thing at the open house. My back stiffens as tight as a board.

Pizza tonight — first time in forever. Halfway through my second piece I'm totally stuffed.

I stare out the window. It's still light, the days are getting longer. The woods in the far corner are a mixture of bright new leaves and dark trunks, and way in the back, the deeper green of spruces. Tomorrow, we'll hide the bottles in the hidey-hole. Under the big spruce.

"You okay, kiddo?" asks Dad.

I nod and flash a smile.

"It's so much excitement, no?" says Nanaji.

"Yeah," I manage. "Can't wait."

Mom turns sharply toward me.

Quickly, I scrape my chair back. I have to act normal.

"Come on, let's get mixing." I'm proud of how cheerful I sound.

Then we're all bustling, clearing up, getting the squirt bottles from the garage. Mom's saved them for years, and we've got more than forty. Lots of other people bring bottles, too.

But my stomach isn't whirling with excitement like usual. It's tight and hard.

The doorbell rings. Jessie's here.

"Hi," she squeals, hugging me.

I pull away. "Come on, we're just about to start."

Jessie looks at me, a bit puzzled, but as soon as she sees the colored powders in the kitchen, she's right into the mixing.

Everyone's talking, laughing. I feel like a robot — spooning powder into the bottles, pouring in water, shaking. Spoon, water, shake.

Jessie's face shines as she shakes up a bottle of bright yellow. "Isn't this the coolest color?"

I make myself smile, but I'm apart from it all. I have to be — I can't let myself forget again.

"I suppose we'd better hide the oil," grins Dad, "in case Daddyji mixes up a special color for anyone this year."

Nanaji laughs. "No, no, not this year. I'll leave that to Mina."

Jessie grins and makes a slight face at me.

I laugh.

Nanaji says, "Anyway, that's not the true spirit of Holi. It's about forgiveness, no? Cleansing."

His eyes are on me.

He can't know, he can't. Even if he suspects, he can't know about Ashley — I couldn't bear for him to know that.

"This is going to be the best Holi yet," I say quickly. "Because Nanaji's here."

Nanaji pats my back. "Thank you, Mina."

I get a whiff of his aftershave, soap. Clean, strong. Safe.

Ashley, tossing her hair back, giggling.

I clench my jaw.

chapter fifteen

Bright sunshine. I sit up in bed and blink.
Holi.

Slowly, I climb out of bed. I pull up my blind.
Not a cloud in the sky. A perfect day.

This is it. The day I get Ashley.

My head's so cloudy, messy. Confused. I don't
know if I slept at all.

I push the hair off my face angrily. I've gone
over and over and over it. I have to do it. For
Nanaji.

I start to get dressed. Last year, I was so
wound up my stomach was whirling. It feels like
way more than a year ago. I was such a kid back
then. All I thought about was having a good
time.

Something falls off my desk onto my foot. A purple card. *The roller-coaster stops and you are left hanging upside down. Miss a turn.* I toss it onto the desk. It's sort of kiddish making up games.

I head downstairs. Jessie comes over right after breakfast, like she does every year. She's just about climbing the walls with excitement.

There's a hard, horrible lump in my chest. Jess is my best friend and everything, but it's almost like we're not in the same world. She acts like it's no different from last year. It makes me feel so…alone.

The party isn't until the afternoon, but for once I'm glad Mom's big on hospitality. She keeps me and Jess hopping all morning with chores so there isn't much time to talk. A few times I catch Jess looking at me, and at one point she asks if I'm okay, but mostly she's too busy having a good time.

Mom looks slightly wild as she flies around, organizing everyone.

I look at my watch. Ten-thirty. The party starts at two.

Mom calls out to Dad, "Don't forget, you're supposed to pick up the *samosas* and the *chevda* from the Indian grocer; I got the *mithai* yesterday."

"Yes, ma'am." Dad salutes.

Jessie makes a slurping sound and grins at me. She loves the *mithai*, the Indian sweets. She can never get

110

enough. I sort of half-smile and head outside to start moving the lawn furniture out of the backyard.

Jessie and Nanaji come out, too. We carry everything into the garage and take out the old tables for the powders and bottles, and a few scruffy chairs. Jessie and Nanaji are talking and laughing. Nanaji is telling her some of the old jokes he used to tell me, and Jess is groaning and giggling. Nanaji's voice is kind of loud.

I run to the enclosed porch to set up the big table for the food — it's off limits for throwing powders. I set out the paper cups and plates — recyclable, of course — Mom insists on that.

Out in the backyard, Jess and Nanaji are still kidding around as they arrange the tables.

She sure forgets fast.

Mom calls me into the kitchen to wash some fruit just as Dad gets back from the store. He's whistling in his tuneless way, carrying three huge bags. I bet he picked up more powders. He does every year.

"Hey." Dad pokes me. "What's with the long face? Hang loose, Mother Goose."

I manage a half grin.

Dad frowns, but before he can say anything, Mom asks, "Arun, could you get me the window cleaner from the main bathroom, please?"

My head jerks around, then back.

Dad returns saying he can't find it. I pretend to be totally absorbed in arranging the oranges in the blue pottery bowl.

Mom clicks her tongue. "Things always go missing when you're in a rush. I can't find my favorite wooden spoon either. Did you put it somewhere, Arun?"

Jessie and Nanaji come in from the porch just in time to hear that. Jessie's eyes widen with laughter. My neck goes hot.

Dad scratches his head. "No. I don't think so."

Mom swats him with her dish towel. "Not that you'd notice anyway."

I catch Nanaji's eyes on me. Quickly, I switch on my smile.

At noon, Ms. Lee comes to the back door with a huge plateful of her homemade eggrolls. She brings them every year. One year, Jess and I ate so many before the party, Mom was furious. Ms. Lee just laughed — now she brings twice as many.

Mom smiles. "Okay, girls. Go ahead and have some, if you like."

Jess grabs one, and bites into it eagerly. "Wow," she says thickly, "it's so good." She reaches for another.

How can she eat? My stomach's a tight knot.

At last, around twelve-thirty, everything's done — even to Mom's standards.

112

Jessie goes home to change into her old clothes; she forgot to bring them. I'm kind of relieved. I'm a bit fed up seeing her act like a little kid, all excited. It's like she just doesn't get it.

Upstairs, I pull on my faded blue shorts and my Holi shirt. It's an old T-shirt of Mom's. I stare at the splotches from other years — red, blue, a bit of purple — where the colors didn't wash out.

Usually, putting on that shirt is a big thrill, but right now, there's just a tired buzz in my head. I take in a deep breath. Not much longer. All I have to do is get Ashley, and then it'll be over.

Soon Jessie's back. She flings a small bag of clothes on my bed — she always stays overnight, after Holi. Only this time, I'm not so...

"Holi is so cool. I can't wait, I can't wait!" Jessie flaps up and down, just like Blither-Dither.

"Come on," I say, abruptly. "We have to hide the bottles."

Jessie slaps her hand to her mouth. "Wow! Good thing you remembered!"

In the closet, I shove aside the basket with stuffed toys. It falls over and Murgatroyd bangs her nose.

I fling her against the back of the closet and take out the bottles.

Jessie frowns. "Mina, what's with— "

"Ready?" I interrupt, hiding my bottle under my shirt.

"Yeah, but— "

"Let's go."

I open the door and we start to race downstairs.

Just then, the bathroom door opens and Nanaji comes out.

"Hey, where are you off to?"

"Outside, Nanaji."

Jess and I run out the kitchen door, slamming it behind us. We tear through the backyard and into the shade of the trees. Jessie is laughing between gasps.

"Do you think he saw?" she gulps.

"Who cares." I push past the lilac shrubs, past the maples, right to the back, to the old spruce tree.

I take both bottles and shove them into the hollow at the base of the tree. Spruce branches scratch my arms.

I get up and dust my knees.

Jessie's eyes dance. "This is so awesome!"

I can't stand it any more. My voice shakes a bit. "Jessie, this is important, it's not just a big joke."

Jessie's smile wipes off. "What's that supposed to mean? And what's eating you, anyway? You've been acting really weird all morning — I've had just about enough of it."

"Yeah, well, I've had more than enough of how *you* find the whole thing so funny."

"What?"

"Jessie, there's a reason we're doing this. It's not just a silly game."

Jessie's eyes flash. "What are you on about? It's Holi— "

"This is not about having a good time, Jessie. It's about *justice*." My voice cracks a little. "And if you don't get that, maybe you'd better just let me handle it."

My hands shake as I push my way out of the woods.

Jess comes behind me. Her voice is high. "Fine. If that's how you want it, fine."

I flop down on one of the chairs in the backyard, my face burning. Jessie fidgets at the tables at the other end of the yard.

I see Nanaji looking out the kitchen window.

I tell myself fiercely, *someone's got to keep remembering what it's really about.*

Suddenly, I hear Nanaji's voice in my head — *be aware.*

chapter sixteen

I sit on the edge of my chair and pick at a small scab on my ankle. From the corner of my eye I see Jessie prowling around. She's trying to whistle "Camptown Races." She never gets it right — she always makes up bits that don't belong.

Part of me wants to go over, give her a hug and make up. But I won't — I mean, she's the one who doesn't get it.

At last, Nanaji, Mom and Dad come outside. Dad goes around to the front with the sign telling everyone to come through the side gate into the backyard. Mom slumps in one of the old lawn chairs and sighs.

Nanaji comes and sits beside me. Why the heck is he watching me anyway? I smile shakily at him, then look away.

From the side gate, someone calls out, "Hello there!"

Thank goodness! It's Mr. and Ms. Lowell. Mom gets to her feet, full of energy again.

Mr. Lowell's carrying a plateful of cookies that Mom hands to me. Chocolate chip and pecan. No one makes 'em like the Lowells. I take my time putting them on the table in the porch. Ms. Lowell's laugh seems to fill the backyard. Her cookies are just like her — big, generous. She loads them with chocolate chips and nuts.

Normally, Jessie and I would sneak a few, but she's hanging around the backyard, trying to act all cool and busy. Well, if that's how she wants it…

I fuss around and try the plate in a few different places — one end of the table, the middle, the other end. I don't go out until I see Heidi and Noelle arrive.

As I come down the porch steps, Heidi and Noelle run over. They're both wearing old faded shorts and T-shirts.

"This is so exciting," says Heidi, "I can hardly wait."

Jessie comes slowly up to us. She looks relieved, too, that the others are here.

Then more and more people arrive. The Rochettes from Dad's work; Mr. and Ms. Thadhani, with

Ganesh, their six year old son; the Stewarts; the Minskeys; the Duttas. Ms. Dutta always wears Indian clothes — today it's a loose pink tunic and pants. A couple of boys come bursting through the side gate — Craig and Josh. Craig's freckles seem to stick out more than ever in the sunshine. He grins at me and whispers to Josh, as he looks carefully around the yard. He's planning his strategy. The pockets of his baggy shorts bulge — he's brought his own bottles, as usual.

Some of the boys hang out with us, some in separate groups. Mom, Dad and Nanaji are greeting the adults. A lot of my friends' parents stay for the party, too.

Craig's mother comes over. She's tall and lanky and real fun.

"Now then, girls," she says, smiling. "I'm counting on you to keep up our side." She bends down and whispers, "Get those boys. Especially my son."

Terra grins. "Don't worry, Ms. MacLeod, we will."

Everyone's so…so lighthearted. I catch Heidi looking at me. I switch on my smile, make myself talk to people. I keep looking toward the back gate, where people are arriving.

"See what I've got," says Terra. It's a bag of bright red powder in her pocket. "I'm saving it 'til the end."

"Give me some, give me," everyone begs.

My eyes swivel again to the back gate. Four people. At last.

Ms. Hughes' face is still made up, but she's wearing faded yellow jeans and a green shirt.

My heart starts to hammer unpleasantly. Nanaji says something to Mr. Hughes. Ashley tosses back her hair and looks up at Nanaji.

An electric shock jolts through me. And it isn't an effort anymore — I rush to greet the anger like an old friend.

Then Ashley comes running toward us, her face glowing.

"Mina, I'm here. This is fun. When does everything start? What's going to happen?"

I feel like I've been slapped. She's so completely forgotten. I start to tell her — how Mom gives the signal after she sets out the powders. Heidi, Noelle and a few others chip in with comments. I still have to carry out the last part of my plan — get Ashley to come into the woods.

Jess turns away when I look at her. Fine. I can handle this on my own.

I pull Ashley away from the others and say shakily, "Hey, Ashley, since it's your first time I'll let you in on a secret."

Ashley's brown eyes gleam. "What?"

Sam's coming toward us. Quickly, I whisper, "I can't show you 'cause everyone else'll find out, too. But that's the best place to hide when it gets heavy. See?" I point to the woody corner. "Way in there by the spruces. It's the safest place. Don't just stay at the edge of the trees, a lot of kids stick around there. By the spruces is best — meet me there, okay, and I'll give you an extra bottle. Promise?"

Ashley grins. "Cool. Thanks, Mina."

Then Sam's saying hi to me and Ashley, and we join the other girls.

There. All set.

Jessie's not with the others.

She's by the old picnic table with Nanaji. He says something, and her face breaks into that wide grin of hers. He thumps her back and looks at me and the other kids. When she catches my eye, her smile fades.

I start to babble to the boys near me, Kev and Steve, but I just want to run away, hide in my room. Be alone.

chapter seventeen

Some of the grown-ups are setting out the plates of powders and the bottles of colored water on the tables. Kids start to point excitedly. Someone squeals.

Then Mom stands up on a chair and hollers for quiet.

"Your attention, please," says Mom. She's smiling, her eyes bright. "First of all, welcome, everyone. It's so nice to see familiar faces and some new ones. It's the Hughes' first time here."

Someone starts to clap — Bruce. Ashley grins, like it's all for her.

"Now I know everyone wants to get on with it, so I'll keep it short. You know what Holi's about — a festival of color celebrated in India. We're so happy to be playing it with all of you, our dear friends and neighbors. Most of you know how it's played, but if it's your first time, just watch — you'll soon catch on."

Craig cheers, and a few other boys join in.

Mom grins. "But in the true spirit of Holi, I'd like you to please remember not to throw powders in anyone's eyes. They won't do any harm but if it happens, come to me or Arun and we'll help you wash it out. Most of the powders and colored water should wash. Sometimes, of course, they don't. Especially," Mom looks at the boys and slits her eyes, "if someone's deliberately brought something that won't."

"No way, not me," yells Craig. "I swear."

His mother comes over and puts her hand over his mouth. Everyone laughs. I catch Jessie looking at me. I turn away.

"One last thing," says Mom. "The house and porch are off-limits — no throwing or squirting in there. If you need the powder room, please use the one by the back door. Okay. I've gone on long enough."

Everyone's eyes are shining. I can practically feel the air humming with excitement.

I glance at Nanaji. He's smiling at me. His gray hair glistens in the sun. My throat squeezes tight.

"Have fun, everyone," says Mom. "Enjoy!"

For a moment, everyone looks at everyone else. Then Craig breaks loose from his mother and, whooping, charges for the powder.

A lot of kids run for it, grabbing handfuls, throwing them at each other. A rainbow of brilliant colors. Others stand around awkwardly, until someone gets them with powder or colored water.

Usually, I'm right in the thick of it, but today I just grab some powder and throw at someone running by — I don't even know who. And I don't care. I watch the powder fly into the air, scatter, a yellow arc, almost in slow motion.

Dad's running around, his face like a kid's. He's already got a streak of red across his shirt. Nanaji's laughing, he's getting pelted by Ms. Hughes, who is giggling. She looks so...human.

Ashley. She's standing around, unsure. She awkwardly heaves a burst of green powder at Kevin as he runs by. He turns and splats her with yellow from his bottle. She squeals, standing uselessly.

Then Bruce comes toward Ashley and squirts purple. Ashley dodges and starts to run, but Bruce keeps chasing her.

Now's my chance. "Hey, Ashley, work your way there. Remember?"

She nods.

I run into the woods, to the big spruce tree.

This is it. My heart races.

The branches of the spruce scratch my arms as I scramble to reach the bottles. I shake them hard, set the sprayers as wide as they'll go, then duck behind a tree. From the backyard come shouts and squeals and laughter.

No sign of Ashley.

I wipe my forehead against my sleeve, work my way toward the edge of the trees. Craig is hiding behind a maple, his usual two bottles in his hand. He gets my shirt with a weird shade of red, but I ignore him. Ashley is coming.

I dart out and aim with both bottles. At Ashley's hair. But just as the liquid leaves the bottle, Bruce gets her, and she dives away from the trees. The dirty spray misses, falls uselessly on the grass.

There's a nasty taste in my mouth.

Bruce is still chasing her, squirting, squirting.

She turns again and comes toward the trees. For a moment, my hand freezes. She's covered in colors, she looks so messy, uncool. Do I...

No. No second guessing. I won't blow it now.

"Ashley." I step out. My heart is hammering so fast, it's going to explode. I don't know if anyone else is around, I don't care, I'm going to get her.

And Ashley comes straight toward me.

126

At last, at last.
I squeeze hard.
As I squirt, someone moves between us.
Someone — Nanaji.

chapter eighteen

It's a direct hit. Over his heart. The dirty spray spreads like a flower across his chest, no like a bomb, ugly, staining, staining. Ashley doesn't even see me, she's running away from the trees, with Bruce still after her.

I'm frozen.

Nanaji walks slowly toward me, smiling.

All around, kids scream, throw powders, squirt, run. Craig is gaping at me. Then someone pelts him and he shouts and runs off.

Nanaji bends down. He's not wearing his glasses and his face is spattered with blue, yellow.

"Feel better, now, Minu?" he says. There's not a speck of anger in his eyes.

"Nanaji. I'm sorry, it wasn't for you." With the backs of my hands I dab and dab at his shirt, but it's still there on him, a slap. "I'm sorry, I'm sorry." I'm starting to shake.

Nanaji puts his hand on my back, takes me into the trees, back to the spruce, away from everyone. My fingers still grip the bottles.

In the distance, like in another world, I hear laughter.

Nanaji sniffs at his shirt. "Oh-ho, I knew you were up to something, Minu, but I didn't know what. My goodness. What is it?"

"D-drink crystals," I manage. "And food coloring."

Shrieks from far away.

Nanaji grins. "Very ingenious.

"It wasn't for you, Nanaji, it *wasn't*, I didn't— "

Nanaji pats my cheek. "I know Minu. But I couldn't just stand by and let it happen to Ashley." He pauses. "So what if she makes fun of how I talk?"

My heart squeezes like it's going to burst. "How...how do you know?"

"I got it out of your mummyji." He smiles. "I can tell when something is bothering my daughter." He scratches his nose, smearing the blue. "You know, it's a funny thing, anger. I've noticed that the things that make me most angry about others are the things that I don't like inside me."

He looks at me mildly.

I stare into Nanaji's eyes. See myself reflected there.

Ashley. It isn't just about her.

Me.

It's also about me. Nanaji's voice. *Me* being embarrassed.

I drop the bottles, and my arms go around Nanaji. I'm crying, crying, I can't stop, can't. It's like I'm seven again — leaving on that train in India, hot dust swirling, the whistle wailing, Dad holding me as I lean out of the train window, try to reach Nanaji, don't want to say goodbye, can't bear...

"Hush now, Minu. It's all right, it's all right." Nanaji pats my back. "You're not the first person to grow, to find your grandfather annoying at times."

"I don't, I don't!" I press my cheek against his heart, press it on the cold, wet, sickly-sweet mess, feel it soak into me, want it to.

Nanaji's clean smell stops me from drowning.

At last, I pull away. I dab at my face with the backs of my hands. In the distance, the shouting continues.

Nanaji bends down, his eyes intent. "Mina, this too is part of life. Just— "

I know what he's going to say, I just know it. "Be aware." I hiccup.

Nanaji bursts out laughing. "That's it."

More yelling in the distance.

I see it in his eyes — how he is aware, and a bit sad, too. And I get a flash of clear understanding — *why* he keeps saying it, how it's a way to see, know, not just stumble along blindly. I see it, but then it clouds again.

The shouts get louder, then the branches rustle and someone comes running through, panting, giggling.

Ashley.

Jessie is right behind her.

"There you are, Mina," puffs Ashley. She's grinning, spattered with colors, her hair matted, sticking out.

She sees Nanaji and looks uncertainly at me. Jessie stares at the blotch on Nanaji's chest, her mouth slightly open.

And I can't help it — I mean, Ashley, she's such a mess, her hair so wild, she looks so uncool, so totally uncool — I start to laugh. I laugh and laugh.

Ashley half-grins, like she doesn't know what's going on. Jessie's face has this *are you nuts* look that cracks me up even more.

Nanaji's smiling at me, like he's *aware*, in that way he has.

Suddenly, through the laughter, through all the mess in my head, I know what I have to do.

Still laughing a bit, I put my arm around Nanaji's waist. "Ashley, this...this is my grandfather."

Ashley looks surprised. A bit embarrassed.

I look quickly at Nanaji. "I guess I should have introduced you at the open house, but..."

Jessie flashes her crooked grin.

Loud whoops from the yard.

Then Nanaji roars, "Go, go." He nudges me, Jess and Ashley forward. "Go on out there — you don't want to miss it all, do you?"

For a microsecond, Jess and I look at each other.

I start forward, then stop — the bottles...if anyone gets them...

Nanaji picks them up. "I'll take care of this. Go on. Go."

Jessie shrieks, "Come on, *you foul wee beastie*, or are you too chicken?"

I chase after her, shouting, "I'll get you, *you lily-livered poltroon*!"

At the edge of the trees, I blink at the sudden light.

People dodging, laughing, streaked in colors.

Holi.

Someone lets out a piercing, joyful, bloodcurdling yell. It's me. I race to the nearest table — there's still powder left.

Craig dashes by and squirts red at me, shouting. He runs away, his face taunting.

"Come on," shrieks Jessie, tearing after Craig.

I grab a handful of yellow and chase Craig. Jessie's squirting him with green. I throw the powder and as Craig lifts his hands to spray me, I grab one of his bottles, squirt him with purple, then run.

Ashley's still standing awkwardly near the trees. I race over to her and squirt and squirt and squirt. She turns away, around and around, squealing, then runs. Someone else is targeting her too — Jessie. Her green and my purple mix into a weird color. We both chase Ashley into the thick of the crowd.

Jessie runs to a table, then suddenly doubles back and heaves red powder at me, and I turn and squirt her purple.

Then Craig's chasing me again, flinging handfuls of mixed colors. I rush to the tables and grab more powder. Ms. Lowell's doubled over, covered in colors, booming with laughter. Gasping, she hands me her squirt bottle.

With a bottle in each hand I turn and let Craig have it. Then Kevin is there, and Jess and I get him, too. I'm screaming, laughing, covered in powder and colored water. Heidi and Noelle come toward me and pelt me with a mixture of colors. The powders fly into the air, blazing, dancing.

I spray Heidi and Noelle, then drop my empty bottle and grab a huge handful of red. I see Trevor. He's right in the middle of the yard, laughing. His face looks — so unsulky. I chase Trevor until I get close, smear red into his hair, deep into his hair.

Then Dad chases me and gets me with his squirt bottle. I dodge near Nanaji and duck, and Dad gets Nanaji. Nanaji roars with laughter and sprinkles some blue powder on me.

"I was saving this for you, Mina," he shouts.

I chase him and get him with every color I can. I spray, throw powder, shriek.

Then I see Mom. She's at the other end of the yard, running toward Ms. Lee, squirting her. I dodge through the people until I get near, squirt and squirt and squirt, until the bottle is empty and Mom's screeching. I get her until I don't need to any more.

My body feels bright, alive, like wind. Everyone's spattered in rainbow shades, you can hardly see who is who — we all look the same, covered in color.

I feel so light, so free, I could fly.

chapter nineteen

Slowly, slowly, people slump on the lawn. Bursts of shouts and laughter still break out.

"I got you, I got you all," crows Craig, flopping next to me. He flashes his gappy grin.

I laugh and point at him. He's plastered in powder and his shirt sticks to him, it's so wet with a mess of colors.

"Yeah, right, Craig — looks like everyone got you!"

Terra suddenly sprinkles us with the last of her red, and I see Ms. Lowell getting Nanaji and Mom with some bright yellow.

"That was the best," gasps Ashley. Her voice doesn't sound the least bit fake. She hesitates, then comes over to where Jess and I and the others are sitting. I give her a quick smile. Why not? I mean, who cares?

After a while, Dad starts to call out, "Okay, everybody, food. Come and wash off before going into the porch."

We all stop at the hose to wash. Some of the boys spray water all over themselves. Craig tries to spray me, but I duck and he gets Ms. Lowell. She grabs the hose and gives him her fake fierce look.

"Sorry, sorry," he babbles. "I was just trying to get Mina."

Jessie whispers in my ear, "Hey, Craig *likes* you."

My mouth drops open. *Craig?* No way.

But there he is, when Jess and I go inside the porch, handing me a paper plate, a funny smile on his face. Jess bursts out laughing.

Craig glares at her, then rushes ahead to load his plate with food.

I pass Mom. Her face is alive with colors and laughter. She looks at me, then at my cheek. Her smile fades.

"Where did that come from?" she asks sharply.

My hand goes up to my cheek.

Nanaji is there. "Now, Sonia, it's a secret. Between Mina and me."

Mom's eyes narrow. She sees the mess on his shirt. Oh-oh. Payback time.

Nanaji says very softly in Hindi, "Close your mouth before the flies get in, my dear. Your father can handle it."

I laugh out loud and give Nanaji a quick hug.

I grab a couple of *perras* and a *samosa* and chutney. Then I get a few of Ms. Lee's eggrolls, some fudge, the Lowell's cookies, Ms. Dutta's *pakoras* and a butter pecan tart. I pile my plate a mile high.

Dad gives me a look of mock-terror. "You're going to explode."

I laugh. I'm starving.

The food tastes fantastic, like it's never tasted before. All us kids eat on the lawn. I make sure to sit away from Craig. I don't think he likes me, but I'm not taking any chances. I mean, it's Craig.

There's a yummy chocolate fudge I bite into.

"Dad and Trev and I made that," says Ashley. She looks a bit awkward.

"It's good," I say. Her face brightens, and she turns to some of the other kids and starts jabbering — about shopping.

I grin at Jess and we both roll our eyes. I'm a mess on the outside, but I feel clean, clean inside. I can't believe how easy my body feels.

"Oh, this is so good," says Jess, trying some hot chutney.

"Hey, Jess, you know that stuff makes you cut the cheese," I say slyly.

Craig makes a sputtering sound and everyone laughs.

Jessie grins at me. "I'll get you for that."

I whisper, "Yeah, well, I'm just getting you back for…" I look at Craig, "…you know."

"Hey, not my fault," she squeals.

After we've eaten, I take the old soccer ball out of the garage and we kick it back and forth. We decide to make teams — with Dad and me as leaders. I pick Jessie first, and Dad picks Mr. Lowell.

Craig shouts, "Pick me, Mina, pick me."

It's way weird. Jess laughs.

"Nanaji," I call out.

He looks so pleased.

I get Heidi, Noelle, Terra and a few others, then I take Craig, too, even though Jessie snorts. I mean, he's a kicker, Craig. Finally, there're only a few boys left and Ashley.

It surprises me to hear myself call out her name. It surprises her, too, from the look on her face.

Craig whispers, "Aww! Why did you pick her? I bet she doesn't know squat."

But Nanaji's hand grips my shoulder and I turn and grin at him.

Then we start. Right away I try to get the ball away from Dad, and he trips and falls over me. Everyone cheers. Heidi gets the ball and kicks it to Noelle. She tries to pass it to Terra, but it goes toward Ms. Lee, on Dad's team. Nanaji quickly hooks it. Wow! Does he ever have fancy footwork. Craig and Jess and I whoop. Nanaji ducks past Mr. Lowell and Kevin on Dad's team and passes the ball to Ashley. Who immediately loses it to Kevin.

Terra groans and Craig shouts, "Klutz!"

"Shut-up, Craig," I say.

He looks surprised but grins widely at me.

Geez. What is with him?

It's a great game. Jess shows off by juggling the ball from knee to knee, then passes it to Nanaji, who head-butts it to Terra, who scores the winning goal. We all break up, shrieking and laughing, with Dad insisting the ball didn't go in, even when Ms. Lowell admits it did.

At last, people start to drift away.

"So, you staying the night, huh?" I say to Jess. I mean, she does every year — it wouldn't be Holi without that.

"Of course." Jess grins. "Dummy."

We drift over to the back gate where Dad, Mom and Nanaji are saying goodbye to people.

Mr. Hughes twinkles at me. "That was outta sight," he says. Ms. Hughes is one of the few people who has changed into clean clothes, but she's still smiling widely. Even Trevor looks like he had a whale of a time.

Ashley. She's standing by Nanaji, shifting around, looking up at him.

What? If she tries anything...

Ashley clears her throat. "Bye, er, Mr....Mina's grandfather." She flushes a bit. "It was nice to meet you."

Nanaji smiles. "You too, Ashley."

Mom's watching. Her eyes turn to me then back to Ashley.

She pats Ashley's back briskly. "I'm glad you were able to come, Ashley."

Ashley tosses her hair importantly and grins. "Bye, Mina, Jess. That was, like, awesome."

I grin. She's not my type, and we're never going to be friends. But I'm going to remember her like this — half-drowned, spattered in color.

"Bye, Mina," Craig thumps his arm around my shoulder. "See you in school, okay?"

Jessie snickers and I shove her with my elbow.

At last, when everyone's gone, Dad goes in to make some tea. Mom and Nanaji sink into chairs.

Jess and I flop on the grass, stretch out, stare at the sky. Blue, with clean, white, fluffy clouds. One looks like a unicorn. I feel good, good, good. Filled with food, sunshine, laughter.

Jess says, "Look, that cloud's like your roller-coaster."

I turn to her. "Hey, let's work on the game tonight, huh?"

"Yeah. It's been ages."

There's a clinking of cups as Dad brings out the tray. He, Mom and Nanaji talk part Hindi, part English as they sip their tea.

I yawn widely. Soon, I guess I'll have to get up and wash off the colors. But not yet, not just yet.

I want to stay like this as long as I can.

Rachna Gilmore is the author of many highly acclaimed children's books, including *Lights for Gita, Roses for Gita, A Friend Like Zilla, Fangs and Me, Ellen's Terrible TV Troubles* and most recently, *A Screaming Kind of Day*. Rachna was awarded the Governor General's Literary Award for Children's Literature, Text in 1999 for *A Screaming Kind of Day*. She is currently at work on a new novel for young adults called *A Group of One*. Rachna lives with her family in Ottawa, Ontario.

"Gets right into the rollercoaster world of the pre-schooler where one minute they hate the people they love and the next all's well again."
- The Vancouver Sun

"Children will recognize themselves in this realistic look at a day filled with problems, but pleasures, too."
- The Edmonton Journal

"[A] sensitive, insightful story of a girl who just wants to "dance with the rain." ...The real draw here is Gilmore's prose."
- Macleans magazine

"In its most literal form A Screaming Kind of Day is a delightful story about a child who wants to go out and play in the rain...While the plot is realistic and can certainly teach children a lesson about getting along, this story is so much more. The text is written in the lyrical diction of poetry. Through the author's clever description, the event becomes a breathtaking slide show...a "must have" for every elementary and public library picture book collection."
- ResourceLinks

"Coupled with artist Gordon Sauve's rich, expressive illustrations, it's easy to see why this book is a winner."
- Saskatoon Star-Phoenix

"Brotherly teasing is a normal part of growing up, but when fighting with her brother results in Scully's being sent to her room instead of playing outside, she rebels. Her hearing impairment and the frustration and anger it generates are conveyed with sensitivity and understanding in this excellent vehicle for developing sensitivity in the very young."
- NAPRA Review

"A SCREAMING KIND OF DAY tackles the frustrations of a young child, and the disruption of sibling squabbles, but in a very special and moving way... Rachna Gilmore's moving insightful text shows us how Scully compensates...The text for this book won the Governor General's Award, and I can understand exactly why. This is the story of a very normal little girl with unusual sensibilities, and one great disadvantage. The text gives us striking portraits of the child and her normal loving family, and Gordon Sauve's sensitive illustrations add their own strength."
- Andrea Deakin, www.shuswapharrier.com